Reading
BOROUGH COUNCIL

Reading Borough Libraries

Email: info@readinglibraries.org.uk
Website: www.readinglibraries.org.uk

Reading 0118 9015950
Battle 0118 9015100
Caversham 0118 9015103
Palmer Park 0118 9015106
Southcote 0118 9015109
Tilehurst 0118 9015112
Whitley 0118 9015115

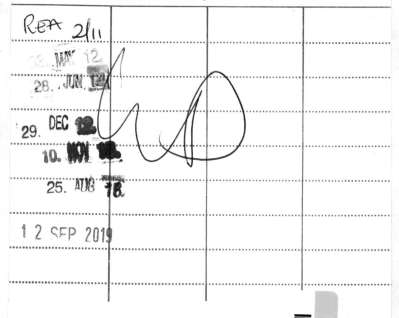

REA 2/11

28. MAY 12.

28. JUN. 12.

29. DEC 12

10. NOV 14

25. AUG 18.

Author: **JOHNSON, P.**
Title: **The TV Time Travellers**

Class no.

To avoid overdue charges please return this b[...]
Reading library on or before the last date sta[...] ve.
If not required by another reader, it may be [...]ed by
personal visit, telephone, post, email, or via [...]te.

KT-449-004

THE TV TIME TRAVELLERS

Pete Johnson

First published in Great Britain
in 2009 by Corgi Yearling,
an imprint of Random House
Children's Books
This Large Print edition published
by AudioGO Ltd 2011
by arrangement with
The Random House Group Ltd

ISBN 978 1405 664707

British Library Cataloguing in Publication Data available

Printed and bound in Great Britain by
CPI Antony Rowe, Chippenham and Eastbourne

I would like to dedicate this book to all the people who shared their experiences of the Second World War with me, and who also took me on an unexpected personal journey.

SOME EXCITING NEWS ABOUT TIME TRAVEL

TIME TRAVEL—just an impossible dream?

Not any more.

Not if you're aged between eleven and fourteen.

For REALITY PLUS, the brilliant, brand-new, 24-hour reality channel, will take FIVE modern children back in time to the start of the Second World War in September 1939. Britain thought its cities were in danger from enemy bombers, so at the beginning of September 1939, over one and a half million people—including thousands of children—had to leave their homes and families behind to go and live in the country with people they'd never seen before.

WHAT CAN IT HAVE BEEN LIKE? HERE'S YOUR CHANCE TO FIND OUT AND BE PART OF A MAJOR SOCIAL EXPERIMENT.

1

FOR THREE WEEKS YOU WILL BE SENT AWAY TO THE COUNTRY TO LIVE EXACTLY AS THOSE EVACUEES DID— EXCEPT, OF COURSE, YOU WILL BE FILMED TOO.

And you will have the opportunity to win a holiday for you and your family at a destination of your choice.

TIME TRAVEL—AND A FREE HOLIDAY.
ISN'T THAT THE MOST AMAZING PRIZE EVER?
HOW CAN YOU WIN THIS FABULOUS PRIZE?
EASY.

Your fellow evacuees will NOMINATE who they wish to leave. But the final decision will always be with the public. *They* will decide which evacuee should leave and VOTE FOR THEIR WINNER—WHICH COULD BE YOU.

But be warned—you will be tested and put under pressure. And during those three weeks, you will not have any contact with the outside world.
So will you be tough enough to cope?
Are you up to the challenge?
If you are, see below for full details on how to apply for:

STRICTLY EVACUEES

EVERY YOUNG PERSON ATTENDING THE AUDITIONS MUST BE ACCOMPANIED BY AN ADULT.

Good luck—and happy time-travelling!

It sounds incredible, doesn't it?
To be honest, it was incredible. An experience we'll never forget. But not in the way you might think.
Time for two of those new evacuees, Zac and Izzy, to tell you a truly astonishing story . . .

3

CHAPTER ONE

How It Started

Zac

I was desperate. That's why I jumped into the shower with all my clothes on.

I stood completely still, letting the water gush down over me. Of course, this made me splutter and gasp a bit at first. But it's amazing how quickly you get used to it. And it's nowhere near as bad if you shut your eyes.

So I closed my eyes—and waited. Finally, Aunt Sara burst in and shrieked, 'Get out of there at once.'

I opened my eyes and announced as calmly as I could, 'I'm afraid I can't do that, as I'm staging an official protest.'

She gaped at me.

'I shall continue to stand here until my one demand is met. And if you try and switch the water off, I shall only go away and do something even more shocking.'

I was talking in a wild way Aunt Sara had never heard before. She thought I was just this weird little mouse of a boy who'd been cluttering up her house since Easter.

And now she was staring at me as if she wished I'd just vanish away (she often looks at me like that) and then she snapped, 'What a lot of fuss about nothing. All right, all right. I'll take you *now*. Just get out of there at once.'

So I switched off the tap, shook my head vigorously and then sloshed out of the shower. I dripped onto the large bath mat.

Aunt Sara wrinkled up her nose at me. 'You really are such a strange boy, making all this fuss about an audition for a TV show.'

'It's of vital importance to me,' I cried, wiping away the beads of water which were still running down my forehead. 'And Dad asked you specially to take me.'

'Well, if he was so concerned I don't know why he couldn't have taken you himself, instead of leaving everything to me as usual,' she said.

'He really wanted to,' I said, 'but then he had to go to this conference in France.'

'Oh, did he really?' she said with a disbelieving shake of her head, which made me hate her so much I had to look away. 'You'd better get changed right away or you'll catch a cold. And no doubt I'll be blamed for that too. No one appreciates how much I have to do. Now I've got to see who can look after my boys while I'm out.' She tutted with annoyance all the way down the stairs.

I heard her ring up her neighbour, where my two cousins—nine-year-old twins who daily whisper to their mum, 'Zac's not still here, is he?' and, 'When is he going home?'—were playing with a friend. And there was no trouble at all about them staying over for a few more hours.

Aunt Sara's phone call didn't even last for two minutes. She just couldn't be bothered to take me to the audition, could she? Although she pretended when Dad was here that it would be no problem at all. Then at breakfast today she'd announced airily that she was far too busy now.

Well, I'd have gone on my own if *Strictly Evacuees* hadn't written in big letters that every young person attending the auditions must be accompanied by an adult.

Of course, Aunt Sara didn't think I had a chance. She couldn't imagine anyone picking me to appear on a TV show. And normally she might have been right. But not this time. Not for a programme about evacuees.

I'd always been a little bit interested in the war years. But I'd become really fascinated these past two months. It had started when Mr Evans had given a lesson about evacuation and the Blitz. And afterwards I'd sat talking about it to him all through break.

I hadn't spoken to anyone for that long since Mum passed away. There was so much more to know too. That's why I started reading books and going on websites and watching DVDs. I wanted to collect every piece of information I could about those days.

What fascinated me was that this was

a war which involved everyone. So I especially liked finding out about life on the Home Front. Soon I knew all about the things people had to put up with: like rationing and carrying gas masks everywhere and bombing raids in London, night after night.

I just lived and breathed those days, until the Second World War became all I could think about. And all I wanted to think about as well. And yes, some people did think that was a bit strange, including every single person in my class. I know they were saying stuff about how weird I was. But I honestly didn't care about that one little bit.

I tell you, these past months at Aunt Sara's—well, it had been like living in a grim, horrible waiting room. I didn't seem to have any future or past. I was just stuck in this horrible, dark void.

I didn't even know what we were doing there, as Dad and I had a perfectly good home of our own. Several times I'd ask him when we were going back and he'd turn this dead, tired face to me and say, 'I've had another very long day at work.

And the last thing I want is to be cross-examined by you now.'

He'd say it kind of angrily too, as if he didn't understand why I was talking to him at all. Since Mum died, Dad had changed so much. He never laughed or had a joke with me any more. Instead, night after night he'd totter into Aunt Sara's house like a weary zombie.

And I'd think, I hadn't just lost my mum, somehow Dad had gone too. I'd get this horrible, hopeless feeling then, which hung over me all night, until I made my fantastic discovery. And all at once it didn't matter how miserable I was at Aunt Sara's any more.

For I'd found a secret door which took me instantly into another time. And it was a totally real place too, not a made-up one.

Sometimes Aunt Sara would glance at me and murmur disapprovingly, 'Oh, he's just daydreaming again.'

Just daydreaming! If only she knew. I was in a completely different era. And I was safe and happy there in my fortress.

I ask you, how incredible is that?

And now you see why I leaped at the chance of being on *Strictly Evacuees*. The moment I saw that advert in the local paper nothing mattered to me more than that.

After I'd changed out of my wet clothes I opened the top drawer of my desk and took out a gas mask. An authentic Second World War one, which I'd saved up to buy.

Then I put on a very smart 1940s hat. Everyone wore hats in the 1940s (and proper ones, not baseball caps. Yuk). And even though it was a bit big for me, it gave off such an air of the past I could have popped out of a 1940s black and white film.

Aunt Sara gave this odd whinny of laughter when she saw me. 'Oh, no, you can't go out like that, I can hardly see you beneath that hat.'

'That doesn't matter at all,' I explained, 'as the hat is of a very deep, historical significance.'

She still didn't understand, but the two people doing my first interview for *Strictly Evacuees* did.

They said three other children had

brought in gas masks, but no one else had come in wearing such a 'magnificent hat'.

The moment they said that I got a real hairs-on-the-back-of-my-neck feeling.

And right then I just knew I was going to be a time traveller.

CHAPTER TWO

How It Started

Izzy

Nearly.

Isn't that the most horribly annoying word ever? It can stab you right in the heart too. So my dream nearly came true. I was nearly on Britain's Got Talent.

Mum and I waited in the queue for over five hours. Then I had two minutes in front of the show's researchers. They decide if you're good enough to appear on the telly.

I'd learned by heart this funny poem (which I'd also written). And afterwards the researchers asked me to stay behind. 'Such a good sign,' whispered Mum. My heart was thumping away now and Mum kept smiling at me so hopefully. Until this amoeba burst onto the stage and started shouting, 'Chitty, Chitty, Bang, Bang.' He had a great pair of lungs on him, I'll give him that. And of course everyone went, 'Aaah', and cried for a week and they chose the amoeba to go on the show rather than me, didn't they?

Just as I was leaving though, one of the researchers, trying to be kind, said to me, 'You did well, Izzy, you nearly got on to Britain's Got Talent.'

Yet what good was that? I think I'd rather have been hopeless and missed it by a mile. I was just crazy with disappointment.

And then, outside the studio, some girl thrust a leaflet into my hand. 'Just to let you know,' she said, 'there are some other auditions going on.'

'What for?' I asked.

'Strictly Evacuees,' she cried.

'Never heard of it,' I muttered.

'Yeah, a few people seem to have missed our adverts. But we're a brand-new TV channel called Reality Plus and we're holding auditions right now.'

Then Mum and I read the leaflet. It didn't sound at all the kind of show I'd be interested in. But neither Mum nor I wanted to go home. So we hopped into this taxi, which we really couldn't afford.

And I went into that interview in such a bad mood. I slouched back in my chair and didn't smile once. And when they asked me what I knew about the Second World War, I was totally honest. I said, 'Not a lot really. I know we won which I'm pretty pleased about. But I'm not big on history, because the past is rubbish, isn't it? And I'm so glad I wasn't a child in the war, because I'd just be waiting all the time for someone to invent computer games and mobile phones and Hollyoaks . . . I really couldn't stand it.'

Afterwards I thought, Well, I've totally blown that one. But it wasn't my sort of show anyway. Yet I got called back for a *second interview. And do you know what they said?—this girl from Reality Plus rang me—they liked my attitude.*

Now that was just incredible as I've got a terrible attitude. Ask anyone. I can get into strops over such silly little things too.

In fact, at school I got into so much trouble I actually had my own desk in detention. No, don't smile, because it was awful really. I was awful: loud and mouthy just about sums me up. And I'm always saying stuff I really don't mean. Don't ask me why, but something just gets into me.

Anyway, there I was back at Reality Plus and two people interviewed me next time. A youngish guy with the mightiest sideburns I'd ever seen, who kept leaping about offering me biscuits and laughing at every single thing I said, and this woman who just sat staring at me. She didn't speak once until right at the end when she suddenly said to me, 'I suppose you'd like to be famous.'

And I replied, 'Well, I'm not too fussed about that, as it happens.'

She looked a bit surprised at this and

said, 'So why do you wish to appear on Strictly Evacuees?'

'Two reasons,' I said. 'Firstly, the holiday—brilliant—and secondly, the money. I know you're not giving away any cash,' I added hastily. 'But I can get rich off the fame, can't I? And extra money would be so handy right now.'

We'd never been exactly flush with cash in our house. And then my dad walked out on us. Yeah, one day he just packed his bags and left. But let's be fair, he did leave us a cheery little note behind the clock. He explained that he'd met someone else, but he'd try and get in touch again soon. What a lovely, caring dad!

Well, I didn't want to see such a hopeless excuse for a human being ever again (and I haven't). But poor Mum really did have money troubles now. So she had to work even more hours at the supermarket—as well as extra cleaning in the mornings just, as she put it, 'so we can keep our heads above water'. I had to do something to help. I couldn't leave it all to her. And getting on TV was the obvious answer, wasn't it?

So when Strictly Evacuees *rang again to say they wanted me to be in the show, I thought, This is definitely the best thing that's ever happened to me. They told me there'd be a ninety-minute programme of highlights every night and people could also watch it all day on their computer. And the whole time they were talking, I kept saying to myself that this couldn't really be happening to me. Only* five *kids on the show—and I was going to be one of them!*

And when I put the phone down, I was shaking. Mum was at work and she didn't like me ringing her there. So in the end I called all my friends and, of course, not one of them one answered their phones. And I desperately wanted to say my news aloud to someone to make it real.

Finally, Mum came home and I thought she might jump about a bit and cry, 'Well, this proves you've got star quality,' or something. Instead, she fell into a chair looking totally bewildered and muttering, 'But why on earth have they picked you? I just don't understand.'

'What's to understand, Mum? I'm special and I'm through,' I said wearily. But she went on looking highly puzzled. And the next day this huge form came along from the TV company.

Mum started reading it and calling out things like: 'What do they mean when they say young people must be prepared to accept the tough discipline of the Second World War? And how is this a social experiment?'

'Oh, who cares? Just sign it,' I said.

But Mum shook her head. 'Something doesn't feel right—and no one's even heard of this TV company.'

'That's because it's new. People hadn't heard of the BBC once. Now, will you stop squawking about like a wet hen and sign the form—or have I got to forge your signature?'

'You do know you can just walk out of this show anytime you want,' she said.

'Yes, yes . . . now come on, get writing.'

And finally she did.

CHAPTER THREE

The Journey Begins

Izzy

'Just remember, watch your temper.'
Mum had said that to me every day
since I got that phone call from Strictly
Evacuees. *But now she was saying it to*
me for the very last time. We were in the
taxi (paid for by Reality Plus, of course)
and she went on, 'If you're tempted to
say something, stop and bite
your tongue. Now, you're not a bad girl
really . . .'

'Thanks.'

'You just don't know when to keep
this shut.' She pointed to her mouth.
'Don't forget, your first aim is not to get
nominated.'

I grinned. 'You really want me to win
this, don't you?'

'Of course I do . . . but whatever
happens you'll always be a winner to
me.'

As soon as she said that, tears started forming behind my eyes, which I blinked away furiously. I really didn't want to walk in there bawling my eyes out.

As the car pulled up outside the Reality Plus studios, the driver turned round and said, 'You go in and win now,' which I thought was really friendly of him.

And there was a large crowd of people watching Mum and me walk into Reality Plus. A few of them cheered and waved, but most just stood there having a good gawp.

'Good morning,' murmured Mum politely to them. A couple of voices replied, but the rest only went on staring at us.

I thought to myself, Just by going on this show I've set myself apart from everyone else. I'm someone different already. I rather liked thinking that.

Inside the foyer a girl took my suitcase, gave me a name tag and instructed me to say goodbye to—well, she said my family, even though it was clear to everyone there was just one person with me.

I gave Mum a hug, and then as I could feel those tears again I gave her a swift wave and walked quickly away. The girl said, 'There's a little reception downstairs for you and the other evacuees.'

'Oh, groovy,' I said. Then she helped me put on a microphone. 'Are there cameras in this reception then?' I asked.

'There will be cameras practically everywhere you go now. Some you will see; the majority you probably won't even notice. But they will be there. So remember—and this is very important— make sure you are always miked up. You can only take your mike off when you have our permission at night, no other time.' She went on, 'Three of the other new evacuees have arrived already, so I'll leave you to get acquainted.' Then she sprinted away while this door slid open. I was standing at the top of a very long staircase. Down below was a very brightly lit room. That must be for the cameras, of course.

So it's really happening. I'm about to be on the telly in some mad, historical show. But what have I let myself in for?

And as I stood there, poised between my old life and this new one, I started thinking, I can't remember ever feeling more scared. I'm going to turn round and run back to my mum instead. Then very fortunately, another voice in my head took over: What are you messing about on the stairs for? This is the opportunity of a lifetime. Just dive in and stop being so pathetic.

I began walking down the stairs when something truly awful happened. Both my legs began to shake. I glared at them, absolutely furious at their disloyalty, but they wouldn't stop. If I wasn't careful I was going to make my entrance falling flat on my face.

So instead I clung onto the banisters and tottered down the stairs at a speed a hundred-and-three-year-old could have overtaken. The three other evacuees, all boys, stood watching me with a kind of horrified fascination. Who was this girl who moved at the speed of a decrepit tortoise?

Then this little boy scampered over to

me. At first I thought a seven-year-old must have run in here by mistake. He came up to about my kneecap. He rubbed his hands gleefully, said his name was Zac and cried, 'Welcome to my world.'

'Your world?' I echoed, puzzled.

He then put on a large black hat, which completely covered his face, and proudly showed me his smelly old gas mask.

'I expect you'll be given a gas mask too,' he said, 'to protect you against any poison gas attacks. Can't be too careful, can you?' He spoke as if the Second World War really was starting up all over again.

Surely he wasn't one of the new evacuees. No, he must have escaped from somewhere.

He darted off and a tall boy with thick, wavy ginger hair approached. 'Hey, how are you doing? I'm Barney.' He leaned forward. 'Did they tell you there are six evacuees now, not five?'

'No, they didn't,' I said.

'They should have done,' he said gravely. 'He's called Solomon. Want to

meet him?'

'Of course,' I said, looking around.

But instead he pulled out from his pocket a sock which he slipped over his hand. This was no ordinary sock though. It had buttons sewn onto it to look like eyes, and little bits of cloth at the sides, which were its flippers. It also had a red, slit cloth for its large mouth, which opened and closed most impressively. Then I heard this high, shrill voice say, 'You haven't got any fish you don't want, have you?'

I said, 'If I'd known I was going to meet you, I'd have brought you something, Solomon.'

'Call me Solly,' said the puppet seal and his head darted forward coyly. 'Now tell me, did you walk down the stairs like that for a bet?'

'Oh, I can see I'm going to have to watch you, Solly,' I said, quickly glancing down at my legs which to my huge relief were only shuddering very slightly now.

'Yes, I can see we're going to have hours of fun with Solly,' said a voice behind me. 'We won't miss telly and the

24

Xbox, not with a talking sock to entertain us.'

I turned round to see a dark-haired boy with sparkling, mischievous eyes. 'I'm Leo, and I'd like to welcome you to the world of wacky weirdos.'

'Speak for yourself,' I cried.

'I am. I'm here because I'm a genius at something.'

'What's that, then?' I asked.

'At annoying people.'

'Oh, great,' I laughed.

And then a shriek alerted us to the arrival of the fifth (or sixth, if you count Solly) evacuee.

'Oh, I'm not the last, am I?' she burbled and then danced ever so elegantly down the stairs. You could tell she'd spent a ton of money on her designer clothes. In fact, she was like a life-size Barbie doll. Even her teeth gleamed and shone as if she was someone off the telly. 'I'm so happy to meet you all,' she shouted as if she was talking to us all in the middle of a howling gale. 'I'm Harriet, by the way.' She went round all the evacuees, all breathy and thrilled. She came to me last of all. 'Fab to meet you, Izzy, isn't this just too exciting?'

'I may pass out any second,' I murmured.

Then Leo whispered to me, 'I can see you two girls are going to be super-close chums,' and laughed loudly.

'Just as you're going to love hanging out with Shorty Pants over there,' I whispered back, nodding at Zac, who was spinning about like a child at his first-ever party.

But Leo kept on grinning as if everything was just one big joke.

Then a floppy-haired young guy in a T-shirt and jeans bounded down the steps and came beaming over to Leo and me. 'Hi, folks, I'm Sig, short for Siegfried, and I'm the presenter of Strictly Evacuees.'

'Hi, Sig, what's popping?' asked Leo.

'Well, I'm about to formally announce the start.' Then he peered at the name tag. 'So you're Leo?'

'Well, on the street I'm known as Leo the Legend . . . and sometimes just the Legend.'

'On the street,' I laughed. 'You little

26

liar.'

Leo grinned and Sig smiled a little uncertainly. 'Let me just shake you by the hand, Leo, and a little handshake from you too, Izzy. Excellent. Now I'd better go and mingle with the others.'

He raced around the three other evacuees—and even had a brief chat with Solly too. Next he got us all to stand in a row for some pictures for the press. He said it so casually too, as if being in the newspapers was just a normal everyday thing. My heart started racing again until I told myself: Come on, be cool, be cool.

Then Sig cried, 'All right, guys, I shan't see you again until the first eviction, but now your big moment has come. So, say goodbye to 2009—you're about to cross over to 1939.'

CHAPTER FOUR

'Even My Name Changes'
Izzy

The next bit was just horrible. Harriet and I were taken into this pokey little dressing room. A solemn, unsmiling woman said she was going to cut our hair. She ignored my protests—said it was in the rules—and soon it was cut in this truly awful 1939 style: so short and prim and with the most revolting bow you've ever seen.

As for the clothes . . . a woollen jersey and a dress that was the colour drab. *The woman saw my horrified face and said, 'You've got to remember, clothes had to be used over and over, that's why they look so faded. But let's have no more face-pulling.' Then she handed me some knee-high, brown socks and lace-up shoes.*

But even worse than all that was the fact I couldn't be called Izzy any more. Apparently this wasn't a name anyone knew back in the dark ages. So instead I had the scratchy old name of Isobel. And there was this big brown label with 'Isobel' scrawled over it stuck on my jersey. I was given an identity number disc to put round my neck too—and told to memorize immediately what my number was (I never did).

Then I was handed a cardboard box which looked as if it was about to fall apart. Inside was a gas mask. I had to try it on. It had a horrible rubbery smell and made me want to cough. But I was told I must keep it with me at all times. So round my neck that went too.

'Isobel,' I muttered to my hideous new reflection. 'Just looking at you makes me want to throw up. You look such a miserable cow.' I turned to Harriet. 'Don't we look truly terrible?'

She looked nearly as bad as me—they'd even somehow got rid of most of her fake tan and they'd put her hair in plaits. But she just laughed chirpily.

'No, come on, we do,' I said.

She laughed again, even more irritatingly than before and said, 'It's all good, babe, it's all good.'

29

I knew I wouldn't like her. I don't like girly girls much anyway. But really iffy ones who pretend to be all happy and jolly all the time are even worse. Still, I reminded myself it was the other evacuees who decided who was up for eviction. So I had to try and get on with everyone, even Little Miss Sunshine. So I swallowed hard and said faintly, 'Yeah, all good, that's right.'

Of course, we couldn't take anything of 2009 with us. We were frisked to check we hadn't, and we were told that anyone discovered smuggling in any illegal goods would be evicted immediately.

We were allowed to take in one book each: they had to have been published before 1939 and a range were left on a table in case we hadn't had time to pick one out before. Mum had given me a really old book which had first belonged to her grandmother called The Family from One End Street *by Eve Garnett. Zac had brought in one of the* Just William *books and, to my great surprise, Leo had chosen a massive book called* Arthur Mee's Encyclopaedia. *Surely he wasn't going to read all that?*

Then the boys reappeared. And I burst out laughing. They had pudding bowl haircuts (although Zac had that already) with their hair slicked right back. Their jeans, of course, had been banished too. Now they had on those funny, baggy trousers which only reached their knees. They wore jerseys too, over dull-looking shirts, and leather lace-up boots.

They seemed about three and forty-three at the same time.

Leo looked at Harriet and me and grinned: 'Loving your new style, girls, loving it. Still, don't be depressed, I've discovered something really good.' Then he picked up his gas mask and blew hard inside it. At once this farting noise came out of it. Everyone fell about. Even Zac smiled.

Of course Solly Seal had to see what was happening. 'Do it again,' he piped up.

Leo had just started his second command performance when a voice called out, 'Who is making such a disgusting sound?'

A very large woman came charging towards us like a mad rhino. She had a helmet of grey hair—and thick-rimmed glasses.

'Come on,' she demanded. 'Own up. Who is being so rude?'

'It was me,' said Leo. 'And I didn't know it was rude, as my dad's always making that noise. You should hear him first thing in the morning.'

I started to laugh and Solly let out a high-pitched squeal.

The woman clapped her hands. 'I shall count to one. After which all this riotous behaviour shall stop. One . . .'

There was silence now. The woman started walking round us, as if we were on parade in the army. 'Well, we haven't got off to a very good start, have we?'

'No,' squeaked Solly.

'My name is Miss Weed.' She glared around as if daring us to laugh at that. No one even smirked, though I longed to. 'And I shall be travelling with you and teaching you.' Suddenly she sighed right in my face. 'I don't think I have your full attention.'

'Oh, yes, you do.'

'Yes what?'

'Yes, Miss Weed,' I cried.

'Now pay attention, all of you, to what I'm telling you next, as it is very important. Maybe in 2009 you've said this to your parents or poor teachers. "You can't tell me what to do. I know my rights." Well, never say that sentence here in 1939, because you don't have any rights.'

I opened my mouth to argue. 'But surely—'

'Not one,' she said crisply. 'Your parents signed them all away. Now we shall set off for the station. There you will meet the controller, Mr Wallack.'

'Controller?' I echoed.

'Well, headmaster,' she said briskly. 'But this whole series is his brainchild. And he is also the executive producer: a remarkable man. Now, our destination is Little Milton, a village in East Devon. We will be billeted at a small farm there. Are there any questions?'

I raised my hand: I had tons of questions. 'First of all,' I asked, 'our clothes, our modern clothes. What's happened to them?'

'They will be taken to the farm in *Little Milton* by Strictly Evacuees. *If you are evicted—or when you win—you may change back into your usual clothes. Now there's no time for any more questions. But thing I'd advise you to remember: expect the unexpected. Now, good luck to you all—I think you may well need it.'*

CHAPTER FIVE

My Own Magic Carpet

Zac

It was quite a long walk to the station and some people were grumbling about that until I explained, 'Everyone walked far more in 1939—as most people didn't have cars then, and if they did there was petrol rationing. Most people didn't have telephones either and even a train journey was a special occasion.' I paused. 'Sorry if I'm going on too much, but I could talk about this time for hours.'

'Well, you just talk away,' said Leo, 'until you notice us slipping into a boredom coma.'

Trying to be friendly I said, 'It's incredible really; we've travelled back in time seventy years—and no jet lag.' But Leo didn't even smile at my little joke. And I decided I didn't like him very much, too sneery. But Harriet laughed when I made the same joke to her. She asked me loads more questions too. I think she was highly impressed by my knowledge.

At the station we tumbled into our carriage, which was marked: FOR EVACUEES ONLY. I gave a little shiver of delight when I saw that. There was a cameraman in the carriage too, operating a smallish portable camera. 'Hey there, how's it popping?' said Leo to him.

The cameraman put his finger up to his mouth and this voice roared, 'You never, *ever* address any camera operator. Surely you have been told that.' Someone had been sitting so still in the darkest corner of the carriage that no one had realized he was there. Now he shot to his feet and bellowed, 'And how dare you all charge in here like that. All go out and come in again properly.'

Even Leo looked a bit scared by this furious character. We quickly exited and came back in very quietly. He stood watching us, still bristling with fury.

We guessed, even before we were told, that he was the person Miss Weed had called the controller: Mr Wallack. He wasn't especially tall, but he had an enormous bright red face with a small, neatly trimmed moustache and piercing eyes which seemed to stare right through you.

He reminded me of those nervous, twitchy dogs which you approach very warily, because if you alarm them even a tiny bit, they'll leap up and attack you.

We sat in a rather uncomfortable silence with just the sound of the camera whirring about. Outside the window though, there were shouts and cries. A crowd was gathering. And then

Mr Wallack told us they were all there to see us off. This seemed incredible to me. 'But they don't even know us,' I whispered to Izzy.

'They know we're going to be on the telly,' she replied. 'And that's enough.'

Mr Wallack allowed us to go the window to wave to them. Leo started doing his royal wave. 'Thank you, my subjects, for coming,' he called. 'And feel free to bow before my mighty presence. Oh no, my mum's here embarrassing me in front of my multitude of fans. I told her not to bother. And do you know what she's just shouted at me: "Behave yourself." What a diabolical cheek. Are your 'rents here?' he asked me.

'My what?' I cried.

'Your parents.'

'No, they're not,' I said quickly.

'You're so lucky,' he replied.

I knew my dad wouldn't be here, as he was in France. And I was so glad Aunt Sara hadn't waited. It made me feel as if I'd left my old life behind already.

But masses of Barney's family and

friends were there. They had even made a huge banner: GOOD LUCK BARNEY AND SOLLY, it said. 'Why have you got top billing?' demanded Solly. '*I'm* the star.'

Izzy (she'd been given a new name—Isobel—but she practically begged us not to call her that), who had been waving to her mum, suddenly turned away and started sniffing into her hankie.

'Crybaby,' teased Leo.

'I know, it's pathetic,' she said.

'It so is,' agreed Leo. 'We're only here for three weeks—maximum. And some of those evacuees were away for the whole of the war, weren't they? Well, let's ask the walking history book.'

That was me, of course, so I said, 'Quite right; they left as children and returned six years later, practically grown up. And when some children did return they found that their family had moved away.'

'Don't give my parents ideas,' grinned Leo.

Then Mr Wallack told us to come

away from the window as we were about to leave. We all obeyed him instantly. As the train chugged off I thought, This train is really a magic carpet, carrying me away to my all-time favourite period in history.

During the journey we were allowed to talk very quietly or do these jigsaws Miss Weed had brought for us.

But only Harriet and I bothered with the jigsaws. Leo watched me though, and pretended he was really interested. 'Oh, nice work,' he kept muttering as I put another piece in the right place.

Suddenly Harriet leaped up. 'I'm sorry,' she gasped, 'but I feel very sick.' Then she rushed out of the carriage.

Izzy got up too. 'I'll see if she's all right,' she said.

But Miss Weed popped up, looked at Mr Wallack for a moment and said she would deal with this. A few minutes later Mr Wallack got up too. 'Continue talking very quietly,' he said. 'I'll be back shortly.' Then he left as well.

'He really creeps me out,' hissed Izzy.

'Don't forget, we're being filmed,'

39

said Barney, nodding at the cameraman, whose face was as blank as ever.

'Oh, who cares?' said Leo. Then he shouted: 'Mr Wallack is just a big bag of tedium, and if I had to look at his face for another second I'd feel sick too.' We all laughed in a shocked way, while Barney opened the carriage door very slowly and looked out. Then he hastily shut it again. 'They're coming back,' he said, 'and Harriet's got a very strange look on her face.'

'No, that's her normal expression,' said Izzy.

The carriage door opened and Harriet sped in. 'Alarm over, just felt a tiny bit sick for a moment, but I'm fine now.'

'Of course you are,' said Miss Weed firmly.

Harriet beamed away, but without actually looking at anyone. I think she was highly embarrassed. I felt sorry for her. I wondered if she'd just had an attack of nerves.

Angry clouds had been massing when we left the station. By the time we arrived at Little Milton the weather had turned wild. Rain splashed down and then thunder crashed so loudly it made everyone stop talking for a moment. 'Very good sound effects,' said Leo. 'I suppose *Strictly Evacuees* has laid this on especially for us.'

'Don't be silly,' said Mr Wallack. Then he announced we were now going to walk to the farm.

'In this?' exclaimed Izzy.

He ignored her. But then Izzy exclaimed, 'Well, I'm sorry, I'm not walking in this. I'll get pneumonia.'

'I don't remember asking for your opinion,' said Mr Wallack.

'Well, you got it anyway,' she replied defiantly.

Mr Wallack started to twitch and looked as if he was about to say something very fierce. But then Miss Weed whispered something to him and he said, 'In view of the extreme weather, we shall in this one instance call for a taxi. Isobel, I wish to speak to you. The rest of you go into the waiting room with Miss Weed.'

Izzy was gone for ages and when she

returned with Mr Wallack she was much quieter.

A few minutes later the taxi arrived and we all crammed in, the cameraman too. Rain lashed down outside and the wind joined in, howling away.

'Do you think the weather is trying to tell us to turn back?' whispered Barney to me.

'Oh, no,' I replied, 'we're going to have the best time of our lives.'

As we drove into the farmyard, there was a brilliant flash of lightning which lit up the whole cream-coloured stone farmhouse for a moment.

A man came stood in front of us: huge and rather forbidding, holding a walkie-talkie. Surely this wasn't the farmer. I just couldn't imagine him living here. But Miss Weed told us he was a *Strictly Evacuees* security man. There would be someone on guard outside this farm at all times.

Then a man under an umbrella came sloshing towards us. He had some other umbrellas under his arm and he handed them round as if they were lollipops. He was wearing a flat cloth

42

cap, and had a gas mask box over his shoulder, which all added to the wartime authenticity. He cried, 'What a night! I want you to know you're very welcome indeed. Now tell me who you all are.'

He listened to each of our names with a kind of astonished delight. He was small and thin, with a slight Welsh accent. He seemed more like an enthusiastic salesman than a farmer, really.

'I'm Farmer Benson.' Before he could say another word, a pig came grunting and squealing towards him. 'Oh, I thought you'd have to see what was going on,' he said, picking the pig up. The pig settled in his arms as he went on, 'This is quite a small farm, but it is a proper working one and I'm rather proud of it. I'm biased, though. You see, I was born on this farm and my late father before me and my grandfather before him . . . and in my grandad's time we had evacuees here.'

'Oh, how brilliant!' I cried.

'Brilliant indeed,' he repeated, smiling at my enthusiasm. 'My grandad

43

took in two boys and they became just like part of the family. Good lads they were, and we've still got pictures of them. Now I've got something very exciting to tell you about them—'

But he was interrupted by a voice calling, 'Are you staying out there all night?'

Farmer Benson gave an embarrassed smile. 'Of course, you don't want to listen to me rattling on. Just wanted you to know we've had evacuees before—and we're delighted to welcome you to your time warp.'

'Yes, but what's the exciting thing about your first evacuees?' I asked.

Farmer Benson grinned. 'I think I'll save that as a surprise for later.'

'Yes, do that,' said Mr Wallack, who had an impatient frown on his face.

Farmer Benson put the pig down. 'Off you go, nosy,' he said and the pig went trotting off. The farmer then led us through a big oak door. A woman's voice yelled out, 'All shoes on the mat, if you'd be so kind.' And everyone, even Mr Wallack and Miss Weed, obeyed.

Mrs Benson was a small, rather breathless woman who seemed to be constantly on the move. She bustled us into the kitchen which was enormous. There was a coal fire burning and a long, wooden table with cakes and biscuits on it. We all pounced on those.

It was then I felt this fizzy, excited feeling in my stomach, as if I'd swallowed about a thousand bubbles all at once. I wanted to jump and yell with sheer happiness. Every moment I'd been at Aunt Sara's I'd felt like a guest. No, not even that, a big nuisance, who Aunt Sara had to reluctantly put up with.

But from the start, this felt completely different. And I knew I'd found somewhere I truly belonged.

CHAPTER SIX

'I Need to Perform Number Two'

Izzy

We were in the Bensons' kitchen, stuffing our faces with delicious buttery scones, when Leo nudged me. He pointed up at the corner of the ceiling.

'What?' I said.

'There's a camera up there.'

I squinted up my eyes. 'So there is.'

Leo said, 'At this moment there's a guy at the control centre watching us, thinking, Shall we put these two idiots on the telly?'

'Just so long as he gets my best side,' I grinned. But it was so weird to think of my mum and my friends being able to watch my every move. In fact, I still couldn't quite believe it. Nothing seemed quite real about these past few hours. Most of which I'd hated.

Yet oddly enough, I was enjoying

myself too. I suppose because my life was suddenly so exciting and different. I really hadn't a clue what was going to happen next. But I was still very homesick so I whispered, 'Hi, Mum, I love you lots,' hoping somehow she'd hear that.

Leo started prowling about the kitchen. 'Now they said there are twenty-one cameras in this house. So let's check out the rest.' But suddenly Wally (which had already become Mr Wallack's nickname) said he wanted our full attention.

Instantly no one even dared breathe—no, not even me. He really was one scary dude.

'As some of you have already noticed,' he said, 'there are cameras hidden all over this farm—with the exception of in your bedrooms and the toilet. They are out of bounds for the cameras. Now a piece of advice: forget all about the cameras. Thinking about them will only make you feel self-conscious and awkward—and stop you being completely natural.'

But how could you forget all those

cameras lurking about? Impossible. And that first night I kept spotting them. 'There's one, there's another,' I'd say. I'd hear the cameras moving too—they made a funny, slithering sound. I got used to them incredibly quickly though. And within a few hours I had practically forgotten all about them. I suppose there was just so much else to think about.

Wally went on to tell us that we couldn't go outside the gate of the farm without permission. Anyone disobeying this rule would be instantly dismissed. So that guard wasn't just to keep strangers out—it was to keep us in.

'You may occasionally be allowed to leave the farm, but you must ensure you only speak to people in Second World War costume. If anyone attempts to speak to you in modern dress, you must not reply but should inform Miss Weed or myself right away.' He continued, 'I will remind you too that we shall be expecting high standards of behaviour from you at all times. Anyone who misbehaves will receive a warning—three warnings and you will be disqualified from the competition.' Then *he added, 'And one person has already received a warning.'*

I gave a little bow in case anyone doubted who it was. I'd got my warning just for announcing that I couldn't walk a mile to the farm while a massive storm was going on. Apparently, I'd been highly disrespectful and very rude.

Next we were told we could see our rooms. I sprang up, but had to come back because I'd left the room like a football hooligan—not like a young lady.

We all clattered up this narrow, winding stairway. The first floor was where the Bensons and Miss Weed slept. The second floor was ours. Two of the bedrooms were very small with sloping ceilings and some distinctly mouldy wallpaper with faded roses all over them. To try and brighten things up a bit they'd slapped up a couple of little pictures of country scenes.

The third bedroom was a cupboard really (stretch your arms out and you could touch both walls). But everyone wanted that room because it was kind of cosy and, of course, it was private. For a few superb hours you could be totally on your own.

But before I could put in a bid for it that seal piped up, 'Oh, could I have this bedroom; I'll share it with Barney if I really must.'

Now Mrs Benson hadn't seen the sock puppet before and she was charmed by it—sorry, him. She even called her husband upstairs and soon Barney and Solomon were doing their full act. Of course they got the bedroom, while I had to share with Harriet.

She had fully recovered from feeling sick earlier. Now she was bounding round our room saying, 'Well, today has been a journey and a half and isn't it just incredible to be here. You know something else? You and I are going to have brilliant fun, Isobel.' She burst out laughing. 'It's hilarious hearing you called that, makes me laugh every time.'

'Well, don't you call me Isobel in here,' I said. 'This is our private place.'

'Oh, I think I should,' she giggled. 'Keep up the illusion.'

'I've told all the other evacuees to call me Izzy,' I insisted. 'And I shan't answer

50

to anything else.'

She laughed again. 'Oh, you are funny getting all upset about a silly thing like that.' She looked at me. 'It's not easy being you, is it?'

'How do you mean?' I asked.

'Well, you get uptight about such silly little things, like your name. Oh well, a few days with me and you'll feel so relaxed and happy. I cheer everyone up.'

Then she smiled a smile which seemed to fill the whole bedroom; in fact there didn't seem any space left for me. I knew if I stayed in this room any longer I'd only say something I regretted. And I just had to keep my temper—as I didn't want Little Miss Sunshine nominating me to leave.

I even had to pretend to like her. So I said, as brightly as I could, 'I'm sure you and I will have a good time together.'

'Oh, we will,' she cried. 'It's going to be so fantastic.'

I fled to the bathroom. Only I couldn't find one on our floor—and then we were called down to tea in the kitchen. Those scones had been delicious and I was looking forward to something even tastier. But a rather embarrassed-looking Mrs Benson announced to us, 'I've been told off for cooking you all those scones. And I can't give you the welcome tea I'd planned; it's all got to be prepared according to wartime rationing.'

'Excuse me,' said Zac, 'but we're in 1939 and rationing didn't come in until January the eighth, 1940.'

'He's right,' cried Leo at once.

'You don't know.' I grinned at him.

'Shush,' said Leo.

For a moment Miss Weed and Mr Wallack both looked distinctly taken aback by Zac's pronouncement. Finally, Miss Weed said, 'You're quite right, Zac, about when rationing started. But we're accelerating you through the war, to give you the total experience. So rationing starts now.'

Mrs Benson actually blushed as she brought in our tea—and well she might. It was the most gruesome meal I'd ever seen. It consisted of scrambled eggs—made from powdered eggs—which tasted of absolutely nothing other than dried cardboard, and then a lovely, big helping of raw cabbage salad.

'There's more cabbage salad if anyone wants any,' said Mrs Benson. I would have laughed for several months if my stomach hadn't been turning belly-flops at even the sight of such disgusting fare.

Amazingly, Harriet and Zac were actually eating it enthusiastically. Harriet said it was 'tremendous'. And Zac said he thought powdered eggs tasted even better than the real ones. But Barney and Leo were picking at their food. I started making faces at them at how awful it tasted.

Suddenly Wally, who was sitting at the head of the table (where else?), barked, 'You have to draw attention to yourself, don't you, Isobel?'

'No, it's just I can't eat this food.' Then I put my knife and fork down and added, 'Now I've finished.'

There was a shocked silence from both Miss Weed and Wally, as if I'd said something really bad. And even Mrs Benson, who'd come in to ask if anyone wanted any more, had a stunned look on her face.

'We're fighting a war,' said Miss Weed. 'Food is very scarce and cannot be wasted. You will eat everything that is on your plate.'

I opened my mouth to protest, but Miss Weed said, 'I am not debating this with you. You will not waste your tea.'

Then Wally added ominously, 'You've already had one warning today.' So I shovelled the foul food quickly into my mouth, my stomach shuddering at every fresh forkful.

When I'd finished Miss Weed said, with a grim little smile, 'I won't ask if you want seconds.'

Potato cakes and jam were brought in next. These looked better, but Leo—who tried one first—whispered to me, 'They taste rank.'

So when Miss Weed offered me one, I said quietly but firmly, 'Thank you, but I'm full now.' And Miss Weed didn't say any more.

When the meal was over I asked Mrs Benson where the bathroom was.

'The thing is,' said Mrs Benson, 'and perhaps you'd all like to know this, our house—in common with many wartime homes—does not have a bathroom.'

'What do you do if you want a bath?'

I asked.

'Baths are once a week. There's a very nice tin bath in the kitchen, and you can take it in turns to use that.'

Farmer Benson smiled at our shocked faces. 'You haven't heard the best of it yet. We don't have an indoor toilet either.'

'I suppose we go to the loo once a week in the tin bath too,' said Leo.

'Oh no,' cried Solly. 'You've got to hold it in for three whole weeks. That's what I'll do anyway.'

Mrs Benson smiled warmly at Solly— he was definitely her favourite evacuee. 'We have a perfectly good lavatory outside,' she said.

'Outside!' we all echoed.

'Oh, it's not far, said Farmer Benson. 'In fact, it's a pleasant little stroll to what we call the lavvy. It's a flush lavvy, as well.'

'And they were still rare in the war years, weren't they?' said Zac.

'Oh, yes, you were considered quite a toff if you had one,' said Farmer Benson. 'But come and see for yourselves.' He led us evacuees and Miss

Weed quite proudly to it. 'Now, just one word of caution,' he said. 'The lock doesn't always work.'

'How cosy,' I murmured.

Farmer Benson said, 'So if you would you be so kind to give a firm tap on the door first. And maybe call out something too. Then listen carefully and if you don't hear an answering call from inside, you'll know it's safe to proceed—simple really.'

'But what about if you need to go in the night?' asked Barney.

Miss Weed took over. 'There will be a chamber pot under your bed for such emergencies.' She went on, 'And if you need to perform Number Two'—Barney and Leo immediately started sniggering—'then come out of your bedroom and say loudly, but without shouting, "I need to perform Number Two". I shall be sleeping downstairs, and Farmer Benson or myself will accompany you.'

'That is so gross,' I cried.

'But,' said Farmer Benson, smiling away as if he were about to tell us a joke, 'I'm afraid toilet paper was not in

56

general use at that time, and we also had to save paper. But fear not, we'll have some newspaper cut up and hanging on a hook by the side, some featuring authentic headlines of the day.'

'So we can read as we wipe,' said Leo.

'Oh, very good,' grinned Farmer Benson. 'I like that—a little bit of humour gets you through most situations, doesn't it? And you are getting the real-life experience of many evacuees.'

'Which tomorrow,' added Miss Weed, 'will include a full day's lessons and, of course, evacuees were expected to earn their keep. So you'll be called at . . . half past five.'

'Half past five!' I cried. 'Even roosters aren't up that early.'

'I'm afraid you will be,' said Miss Weed. 'Half past five sharp, tomorrow.'

'As it's your first night here, we're letting you off your chores tonight,' said Farmer Benson.

'But I'd like to do some chores tonight,' cried Zac. It was really hard to tell who was the biggest suck-up, him or Harriet.

After we'd taken it in turns to visit the outdoor lavvy, everyone—except Zac—trooped off to bed.

Harriet found our chamber pot and Mrs Benson had also placed a china wash bowl and a large jug of water on the washstand in our bedroom. This was for us to wash ourselves. I started muttering more to myself than to Harriet, 'Talk about living in the old days.'

Suddenly I thought longingly of my bedroom—and my mum. About now we'd be . . . but I immediately stopped thinking about all that and told myself I was being a wimp. I only had to stick it out here for three weeks, and if I could swallow a plateful of raw cabbage salad, I could put up with anything.

Then I noticed something hideous, apart from Harriet. Deep black material had been plastered all over the window. 'Why on earth have they done that?' I demanded.

'This is to protect us in the night,' replied Harriet. 'For one little chink of light could guide an enemy bomber to us. Do you understand that?' she added, as if I was completely thick.

A couple of minutes later Miss Weed came in and told us to switch the lights out. And then our room was plunged into darkness: heavy, thick darkness which seemed to loom over me. Suddenly I felt shut in. Trapped.

I jumped up into the bed, my heart racing.

'Now what's wrong, noisy?' asked Harriet.

'Oh, nothing, it's just that the blackout makes this room so dark.'

'People had to put up with it exactly like this in the war, and for years and years too,' said Harriet in such a patronizing voice that I snapped.

'I know, but I haven't been in the war before. This is all new to me and I was just commenting that I don't like it as dark as this.'

Then Harriet started making chicken noises. She really was a total idiot.

'If you don't shut up, I'll punch your lights out.' Then I stopped in alarm. I'd only been here a few hours and already I was starting a row.

But luckily Harriet thought I was

59

joking and she put her head back and laughed. 'Proper little firebrand, aren't you? I shall have to watch you.'

'Yes,' I said feebly, biting my tongue like mad.

'Still, it's all good, babe, isn't it! It's all good.' And she laughed again. One of her really loud ones which bounced all round the room.

I closed my eyes tight and thought, If I were given the choice of sharing a room with Harriet or a family of cockroaches —the cockroaches would win every single time.

CHAPTER SEVEN

News of the Other Evacuees

Zac

It had been a fantastic evening, but the best part was definitely assisting Farmer Benson with his chores.

Cold dark rain had been beating against the windows all evening, but now it had finally stopped, so the air felt magically fresh and clear. And there were so many other smells too all mixed up together, like chickens and straw and yes, all right, manure.

I breathed them all in as deeply as I could, while Farmer Benson told me that in the morning I could collect the eggs and he'd teach me how to milk a cow. Next, I helped him check none of the rooms were showing a light.

'In the war,' I said, 'neighbours threw stones at the windows of people who kept on showing lights.'

'Well, I never knew that before,' said Farmer Benson. 'You're a mine of information about those days, aren't you?'

He sounded highly impressed. And that's when I started playing a brand-new game. I began pretending I wasn't just here for three weeks for a TV show. No, I was a proper evacuee and this was going to be my home for years and years. I loved imagining that. It made me feel my life was all sorted out.

Then I asked a question. 'Earlier, you started telling us something about the other evacuees . . . what was that?'

'Well, it's supposed to be a surprise,' said Farmer Benson. 'But I don't suppose the world will spin off its axis if I tell you. We're having a bit of a get-together on Sunday for some of the people who were evacuated here seventy years ago. And we're hoping both of the lads who lived on this farm will be amongst them.'

'That's incredible!' I cried. 'To meet the very evacuees who lived on this farm all those years ago.'

'I must look out those pictures of the two boys for you . . . although they'll have changed quite a bit since then, I'm sure. Anyway, you'd better get off or Miss Weed will be after me. We have an early start tomorrow, you know.'

I sped up those stairs and was on the way to my bedroom when I heard Solly Seal call out, 'Hey, Zachedimus or whatever your name is, come in here.'

I went into Solomon and Barney's tiny but excellent bedroom (I would have loved that room myself). Barney was in bed. And Solly was perched on his arm. In that dim light Solly seemed more real than ever.

'Now what,' asked Solly, tilting his head to one side, 'have you been doing?'

'Oh, just having a look round the farm. You're very lucky being able to bring Solly with you, Barney.'

'I insisted,' said Barney. 'I said, if you want me you must have my comedy partner too.'

'Actually,' called out Solly in his cheeky, high-pitched voice, 'I was the one they really wanted.'

'I also,' said Barney, 'gave out strict instructions that Solomon must never be put away in a cupboard or a drawer, because he couldn't breathe in there. So if ever he's not with me he must be allowed to lie on my bed or sit out on a table.'

'And how long,' I asked, 'have you two been together?'

Solly leaned his chin onto Barney's hand as if he was about to say something soppy, but then snapped, 'Too long.'

'It's nearly a year now,' said Barney. 'And Dad says I'm as good as most professionals now.'

'Is your dad a ventriloquist too?' I asked.

'No, he's a clown: Mr Carrothead. I expect you've heard of him.'

I hadn't, but I nodded as if I had and said, 'That must be so good having a dad who's a clown; mine just works in an office.'

'So did mine, once,' said Barney, 'but he hated it so much he decided to follow his dream instead; never looked back since then. He has masses of requests. Sometimes he'll do eight children's parties in a week. He says entertaining is in his blood. It's in mine too.'

'So you're going to follow in his footsteps?' I said, fascinated by all this.

'Well, my dad takes me along to a lot of his gigs now. And I help him a lot,' he added proudly. I felt a rush of envy then. It must be great sharing something with your dad like that.

'But I couldn't go out on stage on my own,' said Barney. 'I need someone else with me.'

'Is it hard being a ventriloquist?' I

asked.

Barney replied, 'Speaking without moving your lips takes a lot of practice. Ps and Bs are the hardest. So never call your vent Peter—it will sound like "Eater". But I don't like talking about this in front of Solly.'

'That's because,' said Solly, 'I'm the brains of the outfit.'

Barney grinned affectionately at his seal. 'I really think you are.' I found myself smiling at the seal too.

Solly's head leaned forward as if he were about to tell me something confidential. 'We're waiting for our big break,' he began. 'In fact, we're hoping this might be it.'

Then Miss Weed called up the stairs: 'Lights off in two minutes.'

'Hey, I'd better go.' I grinned. 'Goodnight, you two.' And I darted into my bedroom.

Leo was already in bed. 'Enjoy doing your chores, did you?' He made that one sentence sound so mocking. I really wished I was sharing with Barney and Solly, rather than him.

Then Miss Weed opened our door

and said she was switching our lights off now. After she'd gone Leo asked me, 'So, are you enjoying yourself?'

'Oh, very much. It's just so atmospheric. And now we're lying in a room with not one trace of light in it— exactly as they would have done seventy years ago. So that's fantastic.' Then I added, 'Are *you* enjoying yourself?'

'Very nearly,' said Leo, 'because everything is just so weird.'

I had a feeling he thought I was weird too, but I didn't care. And I wouldn't let him spoil tonight, so I didn't say anything else.

Outside I could hear some twittering and rustlings. There must be a bird's nest above our window. And then a cow started mooing loudly and indignantly. It was all so different from the sounds of life at Aunt Sara's, on an estate packed tightly with houses and people. And me on a camp-bed in a room that wasn't even a bedroom.

It was what Aunt Sara called in the daytime her study. At night I'd lie there aching for my old life and my mum.

The ache never left me either, it went on gnawing away at me all night. But that all belonged to my past, because I was never going back to Aunt Sara's again.

That last thought just popped into my head. Then I said it to myself again: 'I am never going back to Aunt Sara's. This is where I live now.'

I was still pretending, of course. Only now the dream seemed to totally surround me, making me believe the most incredible things could really happen.

Finally I drifted off to sleep. A bit later, though, I woke with a start. I could hear something. I peered into the darkness. Someone was crouched out there in the darkness.

A vampire.

That was my first thought, because I'd had a few dreams about them recently: really horrible ones. Only they don't exist. But someone, actually, was there in the corner of my room.

I slowly, cautiously, scrambled out of bed and edged towards the figure.

And then I got such a nasty shock.

CHAPTER EIGHT

We're in a Time Slip

Zac

I was too shocked to even speak at first.

Then I whispered softly but accusingly, 'You're texting someone.'

And without a flicker of shame Leo looked up. 'That's right; smuggled this little baby past them all. They never looked in my—'

'I don't want to hear,' I cried.

'Keep your voice down,' he hissed.

I stood in front of him accusingly. 'You can't do this.'

'Why not?'

'Because it's against the rules.'

'Ah, but I'm a rule-breaker,' said Leo. 'You show me a rule and I just have to smash it. Now you go back to sleep and let me continue my illegal activities in peace,'

Instead, I moved even closer to him

and whispered, 'We're in the war years now and texting hasn't even been invented.'

Leo looked at me. 'If we're really in the war years . . .'

'We really are.'

'Then I haven't been born yet. So I can do whatever I want as I'm not actually here. Problem solved. Now, let me get back to texting my pet rabbit. He's not been eating his lettuce because he's missing me so much.'

'Who are you really texting?'

'Ah, you're too clever for me. All right, I'm not texting my rabbit at all. I'm texting my mum and dad and bringing a little excitement into their dull lives. I'll text yours too, if you like.'

My voice rose. 'No, I'm sorry, I can't allow this. You're destroying the whole wartime atmosphere.' Then quite suddenly I leaped forward and snatched the mobile phone from him. I surprised myself nearly as much as him. 'I'm keeping this until we return,' I said.

'Until we return!' Leo shook his head. 'We haven't boarded a time machine, you know. You can't actually re-wind time.'

'Oh, yes, you can,' I cried. 'We're in another zone completely. So don't spoil it. We might never get another chance like this.'

'Earth to Zac,' he shouted. 'This is still 2009 and we're just in a reality show—a pretty rubbish one too, if you ask me. Now come on,' his voice rose to a snarl, 'give me my property back this very second, or else.' And he smacked his fists together ominously.

'I'm sensing definite hostility now,' I said. 'Do you want to talk about it?'

'And do you want a smack in the mouth?'

I really didn't. But I also felt extremely strongly about this. 'I'm sorry, but you had no business coming on this mission if you won't abide by the rules and—'

'Shut up,' he interrupted suddenly, urgently. And then I heard it too, a creaking sound outside our door. I hastily flung the wretched mobile under my pillow, just as the door swung open.

Miss Weed, in a big green dressing gown and pink slippers, peered in at us suspiciously. 'What on earth is going on here?' she demanded.

And quick as a flash, Leo said, 'Didn't you hear us calling? We both need to perform Number Twos urgently.'

'Oh, I see,' she replied. 'I apologize for not hearing you sooner. Now put your coats on and then quietly come downstairs. I shall make appropriate arrangements.' Then she rushed off.

Leo stared at me. 'You weren't planning to give me away, were you?'

'No, of course not,' I said. Appalled as I was by his conduct, I couldn't do that. I had my principles—and not snitching was definitely one of them.

'Good, let's get performing then.'

Miss Weed was waiting for us with Farmer Benson. 'Mr Benson has kindly agreed to assist you,' she said, before going back downstairs.

If Farmer Benson was annoyed at being woken in the middle of the night, he certainly didn't show it. 'Now, boys, glad to see you're wrapped up, as it's surprisingly cold tonight. Normally I'd have a torch to guide us—'

'But you can't tonight because enemy aircraft might see our light,' I interrupted eagerly.

'Exactly,' he said. 'So as it's so dark, I shall lead you there and I'm going to ask you, Zac, if you will be so kind as to hold onto my shoulder and Leo, will you take a firm grip of Zac's shoulder? It's a very black night. But don't worry, I know this farm like the back of my hand, and so will you once you've been here a few days. Right, off we go.'

Shuffling forward, we set off. Leo suddenly burst out laughing.

'Yes, this does have its comical side,' said Farmer Benson. 'In fact, I feel as if we're performing some kind of late-night party game.' He started laughing too then: a loud, deep rumble of a laugh. Soon I was joining in as well.

'I hope Miss Weed doesn't hear us,' said Farmer Benson and somehow that thought made us laugh even louder.

At last we reached our totally unnecessary destination, Farmer Benson swung the lavatory door open.

'It's really quite comfortable.'

'Loving it already,' said Leo.

Then I had to pretend to use the lavatory too, and we shuffled back in the same fashion, giggling away as we went.

'Well, it's been a little adventure, hasn't it?' said Farmer Benson. 'Now sleep tight, both of you—and no more laughing,' he added, even though he'd been the one who'd started us off.

Upstairs I said, 'Farmer Benson really is jolly decent.'

'Jolly decent,' echoed Leo mockingly. 'Why are you speaking like that? Oh, don't tell me—because we're in 1939. Well, be jolly decent and give me my phone back.'

'Do you promise not to use it again?'

'No.'

'Then I can't let you have it back.'

'If I fight you, I'll win,' he said.

'I'm sure you will,' I agreed, 'as I've never been in a fight before, and don't know the basics. But I feel so strongly about this . . .'

'All right,' he cried wearily. 'I promise. Now hand it over.'

I dug the mobile out from under my pillow and he grabbed it.

'So how did you smuggle it in?' I asked.

'Easy,' he replied. Then he picked up the book he'd brought in: a huge, fat one called *Arthur Mee's Encyclopaedia*. 'Look inside,' he said.

I did, and then gasped. A massive hole had been cut inside it.

'Took me ages,' Leo said.

'It must have,' I cried.

'But it's a very smug hiding place for my mobile,' he said. And the phone did fit perfectly into the hole he had specially cut.

'You took such a risk, though,' I said. 'Anyone could have opened this book up and examined it.'

He grinned. 'I know, but that's what makes life great, isn't it?' He leaned forward and whispered, 'I'll tell you something else. If they ever find this, I'll be evicted quicker than you can say "Miss Weed rocks". But don't worry, they never will.'

CHAPTER NINE

Life With Harriet

Izzy

It took me ages to get to sleep that night. The old-fashioned nightie I had on seemed to weigh a ton, the bed was hard and, as I mentioned before, the room was far too dark. But I'd finally just drifted off when Harriet shook me awake again.

'What time is it?' I gasped, thinking it was time to get up already.

'Just gone half past three.'

'What!' I shrieked.

'I've been so worried about you,' she said, 'and the strange noises you've been making.'

I blinked at her. 'What noises?'

'Oh, you've been snoring away for ages . . . and so loudly. I just thought you'd like to know, because I don't think snoring is very healthy, is it?'

I sat up in bed. 'Excuse me, but I

don't snore.'

'Oh, you certainly do.' She gave a high, tinkling laugh. 'You snore just like my grandad; reminded me of him actually, only not quite as bad. He actually makes the windows rattle.'

'Well, that's something to aim for,' I said.

'It was my nan who told me you should wake up snorers . . . you didn't mind me mentioning it, did you?'

'Oh, no,' I said. 'And feel free to wake me up any time, won't you?'

'Perhaps if you take a few really deep breaths before you shut your eyes, that might help you,' she suggested. 'And also . . .'

'Night, Harriet,' I said firmly.

Of course it took me ages to get back to sleep—and then I'd just got off when this bell was rung right down my ear.

Miss Weed glared down at me. 'Out of bed at once, girls,' she said, 'and just put on your ordinary clothes for now. You have tasks to perform before school starts. Remember to make your beds before you leave this room, and don't forget your gas masks and that you are fully miked up.'

She scuttled off while Harriet said cheerily, 'You are noisy.'

'Did you hear me snoring again?' I asked anxiously.

'No,' she said, 'but you were calling out for your mum, sounding so desperate. "Mum, Mum," you went. I felt really sorry for you.' She gave her awful, patronizing smile. 'Poor old you,' she said—and her head spun slightly as she said this, like a little wind-up doll.

And then—give three massive cheers—she left. I just enjoyed the glorious silence for a few seconds before going downstairs.

On my way I passed Barney's room and heard Solly laughing. I put my head round the door. 'What's going on here?' I asked.

'I've just told Solly a joke,' said Barney, 'and he really liked it.' Solly was sitting on Barney's arm, his head still rocking with laughter.

I said, 'So even when you're on your own, you two chat together.'

'Of course we do,' said Barney to me in a real what-a-silly–question voice.

'We're mates, aren't we?' added Solly.

The three of us went downstairs to where Miss Weed was waiting. The moment she saw us her head just dropped down, as if her batteries had run out. Then she started chanting this prayer about how we (meaning us, not her) had to be perfect at all times and obey every command we were given by the vastly superior beings known as grown-ups.

Next she began issuing orders for the day. 'The boys will go outside with Farmer Benson. The girls will sweep the floors and stairs and dust downstairs.'

'That's not fair,' I said. 'And it's sexist.'

'Actually,' said Zac, 'I don't think sexism has been invented yet.'

'But why can't I go and milk a cow or something,' I continued, 'and one of the boys do the cleaning duties?'

'Because you can't,' said Miss Weed. 'And stop playing to the cameras.'

'I'm not,' I said. And it was true. I had practically forgotten all about them.

'How dare you answer me back,' snapped Miss Weed. 'In wartime

Britain, children never answered back. They did everything they were told.'

'They weren't children, they were zombies,' I said.

'For that piece of insolence,' said Miss Weed, 'you will continue working for the first fifteen minutes of breakfast, and another word from you and you will miss breakfast altogether.'

'If breakfast is anything like last night's meal, I'll be happy to miss it and—'

'No, Isobel,' said Miss Weed warningly. 'I really wouldn't say another word if I were you.'

I opened my mouth.

'Not even one,' she said.

I closed my mouth again. But while I was sweeping the floors, I thought longingly of the farm. I love animals and wouldn't even have cared if I'd had to collect manure or something. But this was so dull. So was breakfast. Then we were sent upstairs to get ready for school.

Our uniforms had mysteriously appeared in the wardrobe. There was a little tag attached to them too. It said these had first been worn by the real evacuees. *I suppose that should have excited me. But it didn't. The uniforms were so shabby and repaired now that they seemed about as interesting as a used-up tea bag. They stank too: a heavy musty smell. Worst of all though, I just knew the girl who'd worn this last had been really miserable. Perhaps she hadn't wanted to leave her parents or hated her new family. But somehow I could still pick up her sadness all these years later. It was as if her misery had somehow leaked into her clothes. Even today it still hung over them like a really horrible scent.*

And maybe if I wore this uniform long enough I'd start turning into the poor, gloom-ridden girl who'd worn it before. All at once I was homesick again—not for my friends or even my mum this time, but for my old clothes.

'Oh, Isobel,' said Harriet, 'I'm loving this dressing up, aren't you?'

'No,' I said firmly. 'And I told you before, my name is Izzy.'

'Now come on, Isobel is your wartime name and we are supposed to be in the

80

war. And we've got to do it properly, haven't we?' She said all this with such a sweet smile that I wanted to slap her. 'You do make me laugh,' she went on. 'You want to be in the war, and yet you keep on acting like a twenty-first-century child. But don't worry; you'll get the hang of it eventually, just copy me.'

'I'd rather die,' I said.

'What was that?' she cried, a bit sharply for her.

'I said I'll give it a try,' I replied hastily. I really didn't want to be up for eviction. So I just had to get on with this gruesome girl.

CHAPTER TEN

The Taste of Fear

Izzy

Then we set off to our new school. We didn't have to go very far. It was in a barn, where children often came for lessons about farm life. But today, it had been transformed into a 1940s classroom.

Oh, it was dismal: a gloomy little huddle of wooden desks with lift-up lids and inkwells. There was a massive blackboard, a yellow map of the world, curling up with age, and a shelf full of dingy books. Just one flickering electric light too and Miss Weed saying in her vinegary voice: 'Class will stand while they have their hand inspection.'

I thought I'd misheard her. Surely she wasn't going to stomp about examining our hands—but yes, she was. And she stared long and hard at mine. 'These hands are disgusting,' she pronounced at last.

'No, they're not,' I began.

'When will you learn, children never answered back,' she cried. 'Run to the farm now and wash them. You can't have lessons with your hands in such a dreadful state. And hurry up, because Mr Wallack will be starting lessons very shortly and he hates people being late.'

I made as if to leave.

'What have you forgotten?'

'Well, not my hands,' I began.

'Your gas mask!' she shrieked.

'Oh, what?' I muttered.

'What did you say?' she demanded.

'Nothing,' I replied, grabbing my gas mask and tearing off to the farm.

I burst into the kitchen: 'I've got to wash my hands as they're disgusting, apparently. May I use the sink here?'

'Go on then,' said Mrs Benson, and she smiled at me in such a kindly way I wanted to stay in that kitchen for the rest of the day.

I returned to the classroom seconds before Wally made his entrance.

'Class will stand,' he croaked. 'You shouldn't need me to say that.'

We all got to our feet as he flapped in, wearing this moth-eaten old cloak which looked a couple of sizes too long for him. It stretched down past his ankles. But it was what he was holding in his hand which caused my blood to freeze: a cane.

It was very long and thin, with a curled handle at one end. He placed it carefully, almost lovingly, at the end of his desk. Surely he would never use that—not with the hidden cameras on us. It was just a little prop.

But then I remembered that huge form Mum had to sign before I appeared on the show. And I told Mum not to bother reading it all. Did one of those paragraphs give him permission to use the cane on me—just to add to the authentic atmosphere?

No, surely not. Canes have been totally abolished now. But I wasn't exactly in 'now' at the moment. I was in some other 'bonkers universe' or that's what it felt like right then.

'I want silence, complete silence,' said Wally. 'And there's still someone making a noise.' I couldn't hear a thing, but Wally went on glaring around at us. And as he did this he seemed to grow.

No, honestly, he really did. He was like some huge inflatable man looming over us. He didn't speak either, just went on eyeballing us all, while we waited tensely, expectantly, until there was a very deep hush, which was kind of eerie and uncomfortable.

Finally, just to lighten the atmosphere, Leo whispered to me, 'I didn't know Dracula had a twin *brother.'*

But Wally heard him. He must have supersonic hearing. And he half shouted, half screeched at poor Leo, 'I asked for silence, so why are you talking?' Then he advanced forward, like some massive avenging bird. 'You think you know everything, don't you?' he hissed at Leo.

'No, not everything . . .' began Leo.

'How dare you answer me back!' barked Wally. He picked up his cane and pointed it at Leo. 'There are teachers here, young man, who have been on this earth a lot longer than you'—no argument there, I thought— 'and might just have something to teach you, if you're prepared to listen and not make stupid, immature comments all the time. Do you understand?'

And even Leo didn't try and be funny. He just nodded gravely.

'I will just remind you all,' said Wally, 'that while you are in my classroom you will conduct yourselves exactly as wartime pupils did. This means you do not ever talk or look around. You always give me your full attention and you

never answer me back. Is that clear?'

We all murmured, 'Yes, sir,' in a half-hearted way.

'No, I want a proper response. Is that clear?'

Everyone—even Solly—called out, 'Yes, sir,' really loudly.

'Class may now sit,' Wally announced. (Oh yes, we'd still been standing during all this carry-on.) 'And all the time you are sitting you will keep your arms folded. Start now.'

And then the fun really began. Oh no, it didn't. Of course it didn't. Fun with Wally, who just has to appear somewhere to turn the air grey?

What actually happened was that Wally blathered questions about times tables for about two years, and then it was time for history with Miss Weed, who was a slightly better teacher than Wally. But the lesson was just about learning dates from Our Island Story.

And then . . . then I must have slipped into a small coma because I can't remember anything else about that first school day, except that I hated every grim, grimy second of it.

86

CHAPTER ELEVEN

More About the First Evacuees

Zac

At the start of the day a mist hung over the farm, making it seem like an enchanted place. But outside I could hear the chickens and hens clucking and squawking about. It seemed such a friendly sound. And I felt enveloped suddenly with a deep, warm happiness.

'We've landed in a wizard place,' I said to Leo.

He muttered, 'We're on a teeny, little farm, not the Land of Oz.' But even he came and stood at the window with me and peered out at our new home.

Then later, after our tasks and breakfast we all strolled into a real, wartime classroom. They'd taken such care over everything I tingled with joy. It was so still and calm too, and nothing like my old school where the teachers are yelling at people to be quiet all day long.

The meals were great as well and made a change from all the takeaways Aunt Sara buys. So that night we had nettle soup (surprisingly delicious—no, honestly) followed by Spam, carrots, potatoes and cauliflower.

Then, after tea, the big table in the kitchen was cleared and we all sat down to do our homework. It was dead cosy actually and great not to have a television blaring away (there are five in Aunt Sara's house).

Finally came the biggest highlight in a day full of highlights: helping Farmer Benson clean out the pigs. I've decided pigs are my favourite animals ever. They're very like dogs actually. They even squeal with total delight when they see you (especially if they know they're going to be fed). They'll actually trot after you quite happily, grunting and butting at you as if to say 'play with me'.

Barney and Leo were allowed to go in then and get ready for bed. But I was still working away. And Farmer Benson said, 'I'd never have believed you hadn't been on a farm before, Zac. You're a natural.'

Then he made us both a cup of tea. The tea was pretty horrible actually, as you had to re-use the tea leaves over and over. But right then it was as if a wave of sadness had been lifted from me. And I felt so at ease and relaxed. I wasn't just pretending any more. I really was a part of this place now.

Later Farmer Benson went off and found those pictures of the other evacuees, the ones who'd been here seventy years ago.

One of them, Dennis, reminded me instantly of Leo. He had a very similar smile—sort of challenging and very cheeky. He looked straight at the camera in every shot too, as if to say: 'Nothing scares me.'

The other boy was often slightly out of focus: he seemed much shyer, a bit on the edge of things. Rather like me, I suppose. His name was Victor. And Victor stayed on the farm all through the war, not leaving until 1945.

'My grandad told me that Victor arrived here small, pale and a scrap of a thing,' said Farmer Benson, 'but he left big, burly and well over six feet. Wouldn't think that looking at him, would you?'

'No, I wouldn't.' I grinned. 'There's hope for me yet then, as I'm the smallest boy in my class.'

'Oh, there's always hope,' replied Farmer Benson, ruffling my hair.

'Did Dennis stay here for the whole of the war too?' I asked.

'No, he had to go back. His dad was killed about halfway through the war and his mum wanted him home. My grandad stayed in touch with Dennis for a bit, and with Victor for quite a long while. But after Grandad passed away we lost touch with both of our evacuees. Still, *Strictly Evacuees* are making strenuous efforts to track them down for the big reunion party.'

'The stories they will have to tell,' I said.

And later, even Leo admitted he wouldn't mind chewing the fat with them. 'But they'll be so ancient now

90

you'll never recognize them,' he said.

'Oh, I will,' I said confidently.

Leo laughed. 'I bet you don't.'

I grinned. 'I bet I do.'

'This I've got to see,' said Leo. 'And if you really do recognize old Victor and Dennis straightaway your reward will be four squares of delicious chocolate.'

'Chocolate!' I gasped. 'You didn't smuggle that in too?'

'Of course I did. I'm the king of contraband.' Then from inside the lining of his coat he produced a huge bar of chocolate. 'Want a couple of squares now?'

I hesitated. It did look very appetizing. 'No, I can't . . . I don't want to ruin the magic.'

'Magic?' echoed Leo disbelievingly.

'Yes, this is the best thing that's ever happened to me . . . history really is coming alive all around us, and the air is just glittering with magic. I don't want it ever to end.'

Leo looked as if he was going to say something sarcastic. Instead he bunged four squares of chocolate into his mouth and then mumbled, 'Hey, this chocolate really is coming alive as well. It's all the tastier for being illegal too.'

'I really hope you don't get caught,' I said, 'because they'll fling you out for certain.'

'Oh, they won't ever catch me,' boasted Leo.

Only they did.

The very next day.

CHAPTER TWELVE

Exposed

Izzy

And then we had one of those days which just got worse and worse.

It started with me emptying the chamber pot (I never used it, but Harriet did) into the bucket, adding the dirty washing water and then hurling this delightful brew down the outside lavvy. Quality fun or what?

Then Miss Weed told me to dust

downstairs. *'I shall be inspecting the quality of your dusting too.'*

I said—and I only said it as a kind of joke, *'All right, don't freak out about it.'*

But she went mad. *'How dare you answer me back? How dare you, madam.'*

'But—' I began.

'Do you want to argue with me, madam?'

I shook my head.

'Good, because it would be extremely unwise. Now, get on with your tasks without another single word.' Then she added a bit more calmly, *'You really are your own worst enemy. You just won't adapt to the wartime ways.'*

And that's one of the things I hated the most about being an evacuee—you can't ever give your opinion. You just have to do what you're told all the time. It's as if you're not a proper person yet.

Later I had to work out 19 x 12 on the blackboard and managed to get it completely wrong. Wally made such a big deal of that. And I just had to stand there, taking it. Couldn't stick up for myself.

Then at the end of the morning came a massive surprise. 'We warned you to expect the unexpected,' said Wally. 'Now a van from Strictly Evacuees *has just pulled up at the farm: each of you will, in turn, go inside the van. There you will be asked to choose the two people you wish to leave. The people with the highest number of votes will then be put to the public vote and the audience will decide who goes on Monday.'*

We knew there would be nominations, of course. But we'd never expected them as early as this. We were all very shocked.

And who should I pick? I thought for, oh, half a millionth of a second. Harriet.

But who would my second choice be? I quickly ran through them. First, Leo: now, I really liked him. In fact, he was probably the person I got on best with here. Barney and Solomon were great too—and the house would be so much duller without them. I was a tiny bit worried about them winning though. So I suppose I could vote tactically. But I really didn't want to do that.

So this left Zac. Now he was a freaky dude all right, scampering about all the time like an eager puppy about to be taken out for its first-ever walk. But I didn't feel he was putting on an act the way Harriet was. He just was spectacularly weird. Also, it would break his heart to leave. So could I be mean enough to vote for him?

Oh, why couldn't I just nominate Harriet twice?

Anyway, we were all filing out of the classroom to make our nominations when a very grim-looking Miss Weed rushed in. She whispered something to Wally, and then sped off again. He said, 'Class will sit down again. Something has happened. I will return shortly. Wait here in complete silence.' Then he exited.

'What on earth can have happened?' asked Harriet, looking all concerned in a headgirlish sort of way.

'Perhaps he's just found out the war's over,' said Barney.

'No, he's been called back to Transylvania,' quipped Leo.

'Be careful what you say,' I hissed. 'There are cameras in here. He could be watching us at this very moment.'

Then Barney, who'd been acting as lookout, said, 'He's coming back and he doesn't look at all happy.'

Wally came in, looking so grave I actually felt frightened. What was going on?

'I am afraid I have something extremely serious to tell you,' he said. 'Someone here in this room has behaved very badly indeed.'

Right away my cheeks flushed bright red. I just automatically feel guilty when teachers say stuff like that.

Mr Wally went on, 'It has been brought to our attention that an evacuee here has been smuggling in illegal goods, including chocolate and a mobile phone. We have just conducted a raid on all of your rooms and the tip-off was correct. These goods have now been located.'

His eyes started roving around the classroom. Again I dipped my face guiltily, even though I really didn't know what he was talking about.

'Would this person at least have the courage to stand up now?'

Another pause and then, ever so casually, Leo slouched to his feet. He didn't actually yawn, but sounded as if he was about to. 'Oh, yeah, I'd forgotten all about the mobile, but it's a very old one and doesn't even work that well. More like a kind of pet really and we've never been parted. But sorry if it caused you any hassle.'

I watched Leo, amazed and impressed that he could be totally cool at a moment like this. How clever of him, hiding a mobile all this time.

Leo made as if to sit down until Wally barked, 'Remain standing.' He sounded like a sergeant major in an old film about the army. He went on, 'You have broken the rules of my television show! And you're not even sorry. In fact, you display insolence in my classroom.'

My television show, my classroom! Did Wally think he owned the world? Yes, he probably did.

'I am talking to you, boy!' Wally yelled this so loudly he made everyone

97

jump.

'And I heard you,' said Leo.

'Do not look anywhere else, boy.'

'I wasn't,' said Leo.

'You are too full of yourself. You have done a terrible thing, something you were expressly told not to do. And still you're not even ashamed. And now you are infecting the whole class with your poisonous attitude. You are a very stupid boy indeed, aren't you?'

'If you say so,' muttered Leo.

Wally reached for the cane. 'You will say, "I have been a very stupid boy"— now.' He advanced on Leo, with the huge cane in his hand. Wally couldn't really use it. And yet he had such a mad gleam in his big starey eyes, I was afraid. Suddenly you felt anything could happen. 'Say it,' he demanded again.

Leo watched him with a faint smile on his face. He still looked cool, but his right hand was trembling ever so slightly. He really didn't want to say he was stupid, but he was nowhere near as confident as he seemed.

And I just wanted this to stop now. I hate seeing anyone being picked on and

98

I so wished I had the courage to say something to Wally. If he hadn't had the cane, I really think I would have done (I hope I would, anyway).

But someone else was braver than me. Quite suddenly this very loud, very rude burp erupted around the classroom. Immediately Barney jumped up, with Solly bobbing about in his hand. 'I wish to apologize for my seal making such a disgusting sound.'

'I got frightened,' piped up Solly.

'I know you did,' said Barney. 'You always do when people shout at someone for a very long time.'

Wally was watching all this goggle-eyed. Solly hadn't even dared speak in a lesson before—let alone burp. No wonder Wally was looking a bit confused. Then he snapped, 'How dare you make that sound. Go and stand in the corner.'

'What, me, sir?' cried Barney. 'Or Solly, or both of us?'

And that was when I totally lost it and had a laughing fit. You know when you just can't stop laughing. That's what happened to me then. Tears of laughter just danced down my face, and my whole body shook and still I couldn't stop.

It was only when Miss Weed came in with a suitcase that my laughing started to subside. She placed the case very significantly beside Wally.

'He's leaving,' whispered Leo to me. 'Give eighty-nine cheers.'

But of course it wasn't Wally's case. It belonged to Leo. And the thought that he was being chucked out finally stopped all my laughing.

'Miss Weed,' said Wally, 'would you please remain here. I have just reached a decision about my television show I would like you to know about.'

Miss Weed, looking a bit surprised, sat down at the front beside him.

'We had planned,' he said, 'to cancel the first public vote and evict Leo for his bad behaviour. But the conduct of two other people in this room has been so appalling I have changed my mind. I think you can guess which two, Miss Weed.'

She nodded vigorously.

'So,' continued Wally, 'there will still

be a public vote. Only there will be no need for the pupils to nominate—I shall do that for them. I have the power to do that,' he added with a gloating little smile. 'I nominate Leo, Barney and Isobel. It is now up to the audience to decide who leaves. But one of you will certainly go in two days' time.' While the shock of this was still sinking in, he continued, 'As a punishment for their behaviour today, Isobel, Leo and Barney will stay here for an extra hour's work now. Zac and Harriet, you may leave.'

They sidled out, shocked into submission. We remained.

At the end of our detention, Wally faced us again. 'You think you can get away with bad behaviour—well, you can't, not here. I'm setting the rules and I shall break you all in the end. Have no doubt about that.'

I thought that was a terrible thing to say. I went out shaking. And just before we reached the farmhouse I hurled off my microphone. Barney and Leo gaped at me. But it was Solly who spoke. 'Why on earth did you do that?'

'Because, Solly,' I said, 'I don't like this game any more, so I'm off.'

'Well, if you go,' said Solly, 'I leave too.' His head darted towards Barney. 'And they won't want you without me.'

'That's true,' said Barney. And the next thing I knew he'd ripped off his mike too.

'Oh, no,' I gasped.

And then a grinning Leo said, 'You're not leaving me out,' and removed his mike as well.

'I can't let you do this,' I whispered.

'You can't stop us,' said Barney. 'We're in this together—Rebels United.'

'And here's Miss Weed to have a cheery word with us,' said Leo.

Miss Weed stormed over to us, her face bright red with rage. 'What on earth are you doing standing here gossiping? You haven't got time for that.' Then she noticed all the mikes on the ground. 'What is the meaning of this? Aren't you in enough trouble? Explain yourselves.'

Neither of the boys spoke; they both just looked at me. And I knew if I said I was walking out, they've have come with me. Now I've got pretty good friends in my normal life, but none of them would have done that for me. Yet people I'd only known for a couple of days would have given up everything—just to back me up.

I suppose it was living night and day in this strange, historical bubble. Everything happens faster and deeper, including friendship. And knowing I had such good friends made me feel as if I could do anything—including putting up with living here.

So I said, 'I'm very sorry, Miss Weed, we forgot we must never take off our mikes.' I reached forward and picked up my mike. Barney and Leo immediately followed.

I hardly got a chance to speak to them for the rest of the day—we were just rushed from one thing to another. And it wasn't so much the work I hated, it was the constant supervision. The feeling you were being watched and bossed about every second. Not one moment belonged just to you.

But every so often Leo would give me one of his cheeky grins or Solly would whisper 'Rebels United' as he rushed past, and that would cheer me up so much. Now I felt as if we were part of some secret underground organization.

And I was absolutely certain that Wally would never break us.

CHAPTER THIRTEEN

Suspect Number One

Zac

That night Leo started prowling around our bedroom like a restless panther. Then he burst out, 'All right, why did you do it?'

'Do what?'

'Oh, don't bother denying it because that would just be too boring. You snitched on me. You—how did they put it—brought my wrong-doing to their attention.'

I was shocked and very hurt now.

'Honestly, it wasn't me,' I said quietly.

Leo started walking even more quickly around our tiny room. 'Of course it was you. No one else knew about the contraband—unless you told them.'

'I didn't tell anyone,' I said.

'Well then, sorry, but this is a mystery with only one suspect. So, case solved.'

'But I didn't do it. And that is the complete truth.'

And it was.

Leo frowned. 'I was crushed when they said someone had sneaked on me, because although you're a right little weirdo, I didn't think you'd do that.'

'And I didn't. Can't you believe that?'

Leo stopped pacing about. 'No,' he said quietly.

'Then there's nothing more to be said,' I replied, even more quietly.

And we didn't say another word to each other. But I lay there for ages, thinking about who could have betrayed Leo.

I fell asleep, still trying to work this one out. I was woken by someone moving about in our bedroom. He seemed to be searching for something. I sat up in bed and saw that it was Leo.

'What have you lost?' I asked.

Leo whirled round and put a finger to his mouth. 'I'm leaving,' he whispered.

I was stunned.

'Yeah, I'm finished. I nearly left earlier,' he said. 'I'm now just off to tell that SAS man—or whatever he is—at the door that I'm clearing out. And no one can stop me.' He gave a grim kind of chuckle. 'See you sometime and enjoy the rest of the war. Bye.'

'No, stop,' I cried, scrambling out of bed. 'Why are you going right now?'

'I'm going to be kicked out on Monday anyway.'

'You don't know that,' I said.

'Well, they're not going to vote out a baby seal or a girl with a nice set of eyes. No, it's me. So I might as well disappear now.'

'But I don't want you to go,' I cried.

'Feeling guilty now?' he said.

'Not at all. But you . . . well, you passed all the auditions to get here.'

Leo sat down suddenly, 'And that's something I never figured out. I went with this boy from my class—bit of a swot, like you actually, only not quite so mad.'

'Thanks.'

'And I tagged along with him, just for a day off really: didn't take it seriously at all. And when they asked me about school I told them the truth: that I'm always in trouble, although not for anything majorly bad or sinister. I just like messing about. In fact, I've got a natural talent for it, that and annoying people.' He grinned. 'Oh, yeah, when they asked me what my ambition was, do you know what I said?'

'No.'

'I said it was to be the supreme ruler of the universe and live all on my own at the top of a big castle with only two falcons for company.' We both laughed. 'I was just freestyling it,' he said. 'Hadn't a clue what I was going on about really.'

'And only you could think of that.' I smiled. 'But still they asked you back.'

Leo grinned. 'Yeah, and when they

rang to say I'd been chosen for the show, it was just unbelievable, as I'd never been picked for anything in my life before. A total shock. You should have seen my parents' faces. I thought my mum was going to pass out. And for days I was certain they'd ring up and say they'd made a mistake and wanted quite a different boy to me.'

'But they didn't, and here you are on the adventure of a lifetime,' I said enthusiastically. 'And you can't miss what's going to happen tomorrow.'

'Is that when Wally turns into a bat?'

'No, that's when we meet the other evacuees for the reunion party,' I said impatiently, 'including Dennis and Victor. Think what they can tell us new evacuees.'

'We're not new evacuees,' he said.

'Yes, we are.'

'No, we're just playing at it for a few hours for the TV cameras.'

'No, listen, we're—'

'Shut up a minute,' Leo interrupted. He shot to the bedroom door, just as the handle was turning. Miss Weed jumped back in surprise at seeing him.

He was standing right in front of the door so she couldn't see his packed bag.

'I heard voices,' she said.

'Yes, I'm sorry, Miss Weed, I'm very much afraid that I need to perform Number Two again. As you can see, I'm all dressed and ready for action.'

'Oh well, all right,' she said ungraciously, 'if it's an emergency. But in future, just tap lightly on my door; don't make a hullabaloo in here. And does Zac need to avail himself of the facilities too?'

'Yes, please,' I called.

Miss Weed went off to see if Farmer Benson was available to accompany us, while Leo said to me, 'You rebel, pretending you want to perform Number Two in the middle of the night again.'

'I guess I'm getting used to law-breaking,' I said. 'It must be your bad influence. I'll help you unpack when we get back.'

Leo nodded, and then said slowly, 'You really didn't dob me in, did you?' Before I could reply he went on,

'There's no way it's Barney or Izzy either, as they're my mates.'

'As I hope I am,' I said quickly.

'Yeah, I suppose you are. So then, it's got to be Harriet. She must have been creeping about in the night and overheard us arguing.'

'No,' I said.

'It's got to be her.'

'But I like her,' I said.

'I don't. She's too cheerful all the time. It isn't natural. No, she's definitely suspect number one.'

CHAPTER FOURTEEN

Letters from Home

Izzy

Next day was Sunday and a huge improvement. No school for a start.

We still had all our jobs to do, though. And then we had some early morning PE with Miss Weed making us do all these daft fitness exercises.

Harriet, of course, was all red and keen.

Breakfast was so flavourless though. I was eating as little as I could get away with now. Then Mrs Benson summoned me to the kitchen. She said I hadn't cleaned something properly. I was a bit surprised, as she wasn't usually as picky as Miss Weed, but then she hissed, 'Stand right in the corner of the kitchen as the TV cameras can't see you there,' then flung these cakes at me.

'Now eat them as quickly as you can,' she whispered. 'I can't have you wasting away to nothing.' Then she said aloud, 'I want them much cleaner than you managed before. Get to work, Izzy.'

I did. I polished off every one of those cakes and had just wiped the crumbs from my mouth when Miss Weed appeared. 'How is Isobel getting on?' she asked.

'Just finished this second,' said Mrs Benson.

Next we marched in to church. It was packed and every single person there was dressed up in wartime clothes. It felt as if I was in some mad play, especially when the vicar—one of those jolly, smiley ones—said how pleased he was to welcome us evacuees to the village. And he hoped our stay here would be a long and happy one.

The most embarrassing moment was when we sang the hymns and old Wally's singing—a kind of high-pitched snarling—totally drowned out everyone else.

On the way back Leo murmured in my ear, 'On a scale of one to ten, how much do you like Harriet—ten being top?'

'Well, I've just been to church,' I hissed back, 'and am feeling rather kind, so I'll say . . . minus eleven.'

Then he whispered his suspicions about Harriet.

Immediately I said, 'Yeah, it's her all right . . . she's the spy, no question.'

'Well, don't let on we suspect her,' said Leo, 'but keep her under observation.'

'I certainly will,' I said.

When we got back there was a surprise for us: letters from home.

Mum sent me three pages. She said it

didn't matter how well I did as an evacuee as she was already the proudest mum in the world. Total rubbish, of course, but I had to keep saying to myself: 'I'm not going to cry, I'm not.'

In the end I got up and walked into the kitchen. It was deserted, so I took a couple of deep breaths. Then I realized I wasn't on my own after all. A small figure was crouched in the corner. At first I thought Zac was crying and wondered whether just to creep away. But then I saw he was tearing something up.

I went over. 'What's that?' I smiled. 'A love letter from Miss Weed?'

He didn't smile back. Then I guessed what it was.

'That's not your letter from home?'

He sprang up. He'd torn the letter into such tiny pieces that it looked like confetti. 'Four, rotten lines, that's all he wrote to me. He said he hoped I was well and enjoying the wartime experience, and every word was so dead and cold, as if he was writing to someone he hardly knew.'

'Is that from your dad?' I asked

softly.

He nodded and sniffed all at the same time.

'Well, you can't tell me anything about dads,' I began, and then I said, 'but perhaps another better letter is on its way to you?'

'I don't think so,' said Zac firmly. He got up. 'I suppose I'd better put these bits in the bin.' Tears were still pouring down his face.

'No, I'll do that, won't take a second.' I scooped them up. Then I asked, 'But what about your mum? I bet she'll write you a decent letter.'

His voice dipped, becoming so soft I could hardly hear him. 'I'm afraid my mum passed away the week before Easter.'

CHAPTER FIFTEEN

A New Home

Zac

Mum had been away in London at a conference. Meanwhile Dad and I had been busy tidying up the house for her return. I'd helped him do some decorating too, and it looked really good. We couldn't wait for Mum to see it.

But she never did, as on the way home her car was in a very bad accident.

It was horrible going into a house that should have had three people in it, but now it only had two. No wonder it seemed far too big for just Dad and me. In fact, it didn't even seem to belong to us any more.

Then at the funeral this woman started whispering that she didn't know how Dad would cope, as Mum had meant everything to him. Right away I rushed over to him. He was standing looking out of the window and I knew he was crying inside, which is the worst kind of crying really. I so badly wanted to say something to him.

But nothing I could think of seemed big enough somehow. Not that Dad could have heard me anyway. He was far away from everyone that afternoon.

And then Dad's sister, Aunt Sara, invited us for Easter. We hadn't seen much of her for years, even though she only lived a couple of miles away. But then she and Uncle Paul had split up, leaving her with the twins to bring up. And just before Mum died I'm pretty certain Dad lent Aunt Sara some money. But I don't think he really liked her that much. He was helping her out of duty.

I'm certain she invited us round for Easter for the same reason—duty. And I couldn't wait to go home again. Only we never did. Dad went on giving Aunt Sara money, so she was happy. And Dad was hardly there, because he went back to work almost right away, even taking on extra weekend work. Soon he was working longer hours than he had when Mum had been alive. While the weeks at Aunt Sara's stretched into months, I thought: One day Dad will see how I hate every particle of every day here. My old dad would have spotted that right away. But he seemed to have vanished the day Mum died. And that four-line letter he'd just sent me showed he wasn't coming back.

Not ever.

And my new dad just couldn't be bothered with me. I was only a big nuisance to him now. In fact, if he could, I bet he'd like to pay Aunt Sara a bit more money and dump me on her permanently. Then he could go and start a brand-new life somewhere else and forget all about me.

After I'd torn his apology of a note up, Izzy insisted on putting the bits away in the bin. And when she came back she started asking me about my mum. I know Izzy was trying to be kind, but I really didn't want to talk about Mum just then. So I told her I was going to see Farmer Benson.

He was outside and I asked him if

there were any extra little chores he wanted doing. I often asked him that and he always looked pleased. 'Now, what would I do without my star helper?' he said. 'You never stop working on a farm. There aren't very exciting chores though, just helping me carry—'

'I'll do anything,' I said eagerly.

And I worked away even more keenly than usual. Then we stopped for a tasteless cup of tea and I asked Farmer Benson if he had any children. He told me he'd got one daughter who's at university and doing really well, but she had absolutely no interest in farming at all. Then he went on to say that I've worked so hard he doesn't know how he'll manage after I've gone.

And that's when I had my dazzling brainwave.

Up to now, me staying on here had just been like a game of 'Let's pretend'. But now I saw how it actually could come true.

Dad wants rid of me, and Farmer Benson doesn't know how he'll manage without me. Well, he won't have to any

118

more. I'll stay on here after the TV show is over.

And I bet Mrs Benson won't mind either. In fact, only yesterday when she saw my clean plate she said I was an absolute pleasure to feed. Well, that pleasure lies ahead of her for years now.

It was a fantastic solution.

Especially as for months and months now I'd had the feeling that bad things just kept on happening to me. And I couldn't do anything about them.

Now at last I could do something, starting with me living on this farm as a new evacuee. Not that I'd tell anyone just yet. But still, I knew all about it, so it was a bit like having a secret identity, like being Batman or someone.

I sailed off to the evacuees' reunion, happier than I'd felt for months.

CHAPTER SIXTEEN

A Reunion—and a Warning

Zac

Two minutes to four at the village hall.

The tables were laden with wartime food and tea urns, behind which sat women from the village, all dressed in the clothes their grandmothers would have worn. Flags streamed across the room and wartime posters too, urging people to *Dig for Victory* and warning them that *Careless Talk Cost Lives*.

And Mr Wallack had just given us our briefing. 'Remember, this afternoon is about celebrating the real-life evacuees. I shall walk amongst them, encouraging them to tell me their stories. As will Miss Weed and Farmer Benson. Your job is just to offer our guests food: nothing else. You are certainly not here to enjoy yourselves. There are about thirty guest evacuees expected, so on no account are you to touch the food. None of it is for you.'

Then he and Miss Weed gave us a masterclass on the correct way to hold a tray and address our guests. But for once I was hardly listening. I was too busy imagining those evacuees returning to the village hall they'd first walked into seventy years ago. And especially Victor and Dennis. I kept studying their picture.

'They'll have changed a tiny bit, you know,' said Leo.

'Or maybe they won't,' said Barney. 'Maybe they'll look exactly as they did in 1939. Wouldn't that be spooky?'

The doors opened and two people appeared: a woman in red tinted glasses and with two ribbons in her hair, and a bald man, leaning heavily on a stick. The woman announced to no one in particular, 'I knew we'd be the first.'

'Better than being late,' said the man. 'Being early shows respect.'

Leo whispered to me, 'So is he Victor or Dennis?'

'Don't think so,' I said firmly. 'Well,

he's too small to be Victor, who's over six feet.'

'Old people shrink though,' said Barney.

'No, they don't,' cried Izzy.

'Yes, they do,' cried Barney. 'It's a known medical fact.'

Izzy cried, 'So one morning they just wake up two inches shorter and find none of their trousers fit them any more?'

'No, it happens very gradually,' said Barney.

'So if you're very, very old you're going to be a midget,' said Izzy.

'What about me?' I cried. 'I'm a midget already.' They all laughed at that. Then Harriet rushed over to the couple with her tray of wartime food.

'Trust her to get in first,' murmured Izzy.

But a couple of minutes later Harriet sped over to me. 'Now, that was incredible. That woman, Nora, said she hadn't been back here since 1941 when she was called home. And her last memory is of being in this very hall, watching a Christmas panto of

Pinocchio. She said that seeing us all dressed up took her right back. And she could remember again how much she missed her family and home. She said the pain was like a toothache which never went away. She missed them every single day.'

Harriet stopped. She was really moved by what Nora had told her. It was genuine, I could tell. And despite what the other evacuees said, I still liked her. In fact, I felt—although Leo would laugh if I said this aloud—that Harriet was looking out for me.

Then another evacuee strode in. He was wearing a sort of half-cape round his shoulders, had a heavy-jowled face and one of those voices which carried. Leo looked at me; I shook my head. He was tall, but he didn't look at all how I'd imagined Victor.

Leo rushed over to him with a tray of food. He refused the Spam sandwiches: 'I couldn't stand Spam then—and certainly have no intention of eating it now.' Then in answer to Leo's question his voice rang across the room, 'I lived above a sweet shop with some charming people—not amongst the world's brightest, but they meant very well.'

Leo grinned at me and mouthed, 'You're right, he's not Victor.'

Then the man who wasn't Victor turned to Nora and the guy with the stick and proclaimed, 'Well, here are two more people who aren't dead yet then. Should I know you at all?'

Moments later another man came in quite shyly. He was tall and wearing a tweed jacket which looked quite old and probably didn't fit him as well as it once did. He had blue eyes, a wispy grey moustache and quite thick white hair. And right then I knew, I just knew, this was Victor.

I charged over to him, the sandwiches on my tray jumping about excitedly. 'Hello there,' I said, and smiled eagerly at him.

He stared blankly at me for a moment, then inclined his face in my direction and cupped his ear. 'Excuse me leaning towards you in this rather sinister fashion, but I've forgotten my hearing aid. Well, it keeps singing, you see, and I really don't like that.' Then he lowered his voice. 'This is a television programme, isn't it?'

'Yes, *Strictly Evacuees*,' I said.

He nodded. 'That explains why you're done up like that.' He sounded disapproving. 'I suppose there are television cameras beaming down on us at this very moment.' I nodded and he went on, 'Too much surveillance today, cameras everywhere. Whatever happened to our right to privacy?'

He looked positively gloomy now. So to brighten things up I said, 'Why don't you kindly help yourself to a sandwich, Victor?'

His name just slipped out. But he heard that all right. 'Now, how on earth do you know what my name is?'

'Well, actually,' I said, 'I'm your successor.'

'My what?' he said, leaning towards me again. 'I'm afraid you'll have to bellow.'

'I'm one of the new evacuees.'

He still looked puzzled.

'There are five of us staying at exactly the same farm as you did.

125

That's why I call us the new evacuees. And it's a total honour to be following in your footsteps.' Then I added, 'I've been looking at some pictures of you actually.'

'Of me?' he exclaimed

'Yes. Would you care at all to see one?'

He smiled faintly. 'I think I can stand the shock.'

Then I started searching through my pockets for the photo, which is not easy to do when you're also balancing a tray of sandwiches. So Victor very kindly offered to hold the tray for me. I found it right away then.

'Forgot my glasses too,' he said, holding the picture up to the end of his nose. Then he just stared and stared at it. Finally he took a deep breath, like a diver who'd come up from the very bottom of the sea. 'Now my memory is awful these days, but you know, I really can remember every detail of when that picture was taken.'

'That's incredible,' I said. 'The other boy is called Dennis, isn't he?'

'That's right, great chap although he

126

could be a little terror. Well, we both could and neither of us really understood what evacuation was all about at first. I even packed my bucket; I thought I was going to the seaside.'

I grinned.

Victor went on. 'We were piled onto this train—thousands and thousands of us children—each given a green carrier bag containing our rations for forty-eight hours. There was a tin of meat, I remember, a bar of chocolate and two whole packets of biscuits. Then Dennis and I were billeted onto the farm, scared out of our wits by the sight of cows at first. Well, we were both city boys. But we were spoilt to blazes on that farm. Had a glorious time until Dennis got called back; his father had died in action and his mum wanted him home.'

'You must have missed him,' I said.

'I should say I did,' replied Victor. 'We wrote letters for a bit, but then we lost touch.'

'That's a shame,' I said.

'You've got to remember, it was much harder to keep in contact way back then. No emails or even phones for most of us. I've never forgotten him, though. In fact, he's the only reason I'm here tonight. I'd give anything to clap eyes on him again.'

'Well, he has certainly been invited,' I said.

Victor beamed hopefully at me. And suddenly we were both so excited, and the war seemed incredibly close to me. I mean, it was there in the history books, impossibly far away. Yet it was here right in this room too. That was such a strange feeling.

'I've so many questions . . .' I began.

Suddenly a harsh, angry voice cut through our conversation. 'Zac, what on earth are you doing?' It was Mr Wallack, his voice positively shaking with fury. 'How dare you ask one of our guests to hold the tray for you.'

I'd been so intent on what Victor was saying, I'd completely forgotten he was still holding the tray of sandwiches. I'd just stopped seeing it—and I think Victor had too.

'I'm very sorry,' I began, stepping forward to take the tray.

But then, to my total amazement, Victor yanked the tray away from me and thrust it at Mr Wallack. 'How about if you make yourself useful and hand round some sandwiches for five minutes, while I carry on talking to this young man here? We were having a very interesting conversation actually, which unfortunately you've just interrupted.'

Mr Wallack's face actually spun with shock. I don't think anyone had ever spoken to him in his life like that before. But he didn't say another word. Instead, he walked away, still holding the tray very gingerly, as if expecting it to explode at any second.

I watched all this open-mouthed. But Leo rushed over. 'Excuse me, sir,' he said to Victor, 'but may I shake you by the hand as you've just made me very happy.'

Victor, grinning a little, shook hands with Leo. 'Well, when I was a lad,' he said, 'I got so weary of being ordered about by teachers—and we had some right tartars too. I had to put up with it then—but not now.'

'Good for you,' grinned Leo.

Then I told Leo who Victor was, though Leo said he'd sort of guessed already. And Farmer Benson also came over. He said he was absolutely delighted to meet Victor. But when we asked about Dennis, Farmer Benson's face darkened, and he said, 'Let us all sit down over here,' including me in the invitation—and pointed to some chairs by the long table of food.

The room was filling up now, but we were the only ones sitting down. And I had a feeling from Farmer Benson's face that it wasn't good news about Dennis.

And it wasn't.

His wife had rung up to say that Dennis had died in 2003.

Victor sat very still for a few moments. 'I should have tried to get in touch with him before—meant to, so many times.' He blew his nose and then apologized for being 'very silly'.

Farmer Benson said gently, 'Dennis's wife told me that he had often spoken of you, and very warmly. She'd love to speak to you, so if you'd care to give her a call . . . ? I have her number here.'

'Yes, I would,' said Victor. 'Thank you.' And then he added sadly, 'Well, he'll just have to go on living in my memory.'

For the rest of the time I didn't hand round another sandwich. I spent all the time talking to Victor. It was a bit naughty of me really. But neither Mr Wallack nor Miss Weed came near us. Victor was just brimming with stories. And he was amazed by my knowledge of the Second World War.

Leo, overhearing all this as he whirled past, said, 'Oh, Zac here would like to bypass the present and live in the war years, wouldn't you?'

'I certainly would,' I said.

'In fact, if there was a train taking people to 1939, Zac would be the first one aboard—and he'd never want to come back,' said Leo.

As Leo went off again Victor said, 'But surely you'd want to return to your family.'

'Actually, I wouldn't,' I said. 'I'd much rather live here, in the war.'

'Sounds to me as if you're trying to escape from something,' said Victor.

'Oh, no,' I said. 'It's just I don't like my current life very much, so I've gone off and discovered a much better one here instead. So I'm a new evacuee, although not experiencing any of the awful hardships you had, of course.'

'Actually,' said Victor, 'I'd say every age has its own special hardships for children. So today you all seem to take so many exams, which feels like a terrible burden to me. And why have children got to be assessed and graded every second of their lives anyway? Weighing a pig frequently doesn't make it any fatter.'

'Victor for Prime Minister,' grinned Leo, who'd overheard the last bit. 'I'd vote for you.'

'And so would I,' I cried.

As Victor was leaving, Farmer Benson rushed up and invited him round for tea on Wednesday.

'Say yes,' I urged.

Victor grinned and said, 'Well, why not.' Then he said how this had been a very sad day hearing about his old friend, but a happy one too, as he'd made a new friend.

And so had I.

The original evacuees were streaming out when one sneaked over to Leo and me. She said softly, 'Are there cameras round here?'

'Yeah, probably,' began Leo.

'Oh well, I'll risk it,' she said, her teeth jumping out of bright red lips every time she spoke, 'as I'm not supposed to do this.' She moved even closer to us. 'But I've been watching you on the telly every night and wanted to warn you both, and especially you,' she said, nodding at Leo.

'Warn me about what?' asked Leo, looking positively startled now.

'Be very very careful when—' But before she could say another word Miss Weed appeared. She was smiling, but the smile never reached her eyes.

'Now come on, what's this? You know it's forbidden to talk to our evacuees about the show, don't you?' She gave an exaggerated laugh and went on, 'That was made quite clear to you in our instruction sheet before you

133

were allowed admittance. And you wouldn't want to get Leo disqualified, would you?'

'No, of course not,' said the poor woman, her face nearly as red as her lipstick now.

'Now, let me help you out,' said Miss Weed. I looked up to see Mr Wallack hovering close by too, and both of them practically frogmarched the woman out of the hall.

'What was she trying to warn us about?' demanded Leo. 'It could be anything; maybe she was going to warn us not to talk to Harriet.'

'I don't think so,' I said at once.

'Well, we'll never know as Wally has probably had that poor woman vaporized by now.'

CHAPTER SEVENTEEN

The Sirens Wail

Izzy

You won't believe this.

I didn't at first.

But I really enjoyed meeting those ancient evacuees. And I'd been dreading having to listen to them ramble on.

Yet it wasn't like that at all. I suppose I knew a bit about what they were talking about. So when they moaned on, for instance, about how awful Spam tasted, I could join in.

They were dead funny too. This one old lady, Nora, even told me of the time she bit a teacher. She goes: 'Well, the teacher kept on saying I had nits and I wasn't having that. So when she came near me I bit her.'

But Nora got two strokes of the cane for doing that; right on her hands too. Just about everyone I'd spoken to had been caned for something.

You know something else. I'd say meeting Nora and all the others was the highlight of Strictly Evacuees *for me. That, and getting to know Leo, Zac, Barney and Solly. (And yes, you've noticed who I missed out.)*

Actually, nothing was ever as good on the show after that afternoon. In fact, things started to go downhill pretty rapidly, although we had a wild time that evening.

Farmer Benson and his wife wanted to show us a typical family night in during the war. So we all piled into the sitting room and spent the evening playing board games for the undead, and then singing old wartime songs— with Mrs Benson pounding away on the piano. Scarily, I actually enjoyed all that too (not that I'd want to do it too often, though).

But I really felt like a time traveller that night. In fact, I'd got so into the wartime spirit that even when I was asleep I could hear an air-raid siren: a horrible, wailing noise it was. 'Switch it down,' I muttered. Then I opened my eyes to see Miss Weed's nostrils flaring down at me.

'Grab a blanket, some shoes and your mike, and move, move, move,' she cried.

I shook my head. Was I still dreaming? And was I really in the war or not? I was so disorientated that I wasn't completely sure for a few seconds.

'Come on, Isobel,' urged Miss Weed. 'Can't you hear the air-raid siren? Now, move.'

Then I heard Harriet say, 'Don't worry, Miss Weed, I'll look after her,' in such a smug, aren't-I-wonderful voice that I woke up then all right. In fact, I jumped out of bed searching frantically for my shoes, while that siren seemed to be getting even louder.

'My shoes have walked off somewhere,' I muttered. 'You haven't seen them, have you?'

'They'll be just where you left them,' said Harriet, patting her hair in the mirror.

'Thank you for those very wise words,' I muttered.

Finally I found them (and they had magically moved themselves) and tumbled downstairs after Harriet.

Everyone else was already there, except for Farmer Benson and Zac, who were checking all the animals were safe. Then Miss Weed screeched, 'Isobel, where's your gas mask?'

'Oh, will I need it?' I asked.

'Yes!' Miss Weed screamed.

So I sped upstairs, grabbed the gas mask—which was practically falling to pieces now—and tore back down again.

Farmer Benson and Zac had now appeared. 'Sorry to get you out of bed like this,' said Farmer Benson. 'Been a bit of a shock to me too,' he added, half under his breath, 'but there's a little aerial disturbance coming up, apparently. So it's best if we all take shelter in the safest place of the house—down in the cellar.'

'And very quickly please,' added Miss Weed. She seemed really worked up. And although it sounds mad, part of me was oddly scared too.

I said to Farmer Benson, 'But this

138

isn't right, we moved to the country to escape the bombing.'

'Ah, but there were stray attacks outside the cities as well,' he said. 'Well, we had one here. I remember my grandad telling me about a large land mine that came down one night in a field. Very luckily it got caught in a tree, because if it had hit the ground and exploded . . .'

Farmer Benson shook his head. And then Mrs Benson told us how her grandmother woke up one night in the war to find a wall of her bedroom had just disappeared, thanks to a bombing raid.

'I'd be furious about that,' said Leo, 'as I hate anyone coming into my bedroom.' I tried to laugh, but I just felt so muddled too and half still in a dream. Perhaps that's why I was actually scared as well.

We were led into this cellar, which was very cold and very dark and very small. And then we heard the whistle and scream of a bomb falling. It was so loud I actually ducked, making Leo and Barney fall about laughing.

'That was close,' murmured Miss Weed.

But then came the whistle of another bomb, which sounded even louder and felt as if it made the whole house shake. I whispered to Leo, 'They're not really going to blow us up, are they?'

'If it improves the ratings, they will,' he replied. 'But no, it's *not* really *real*; it's just to wind us up. There's a little camera hidden up there.'

And I knew that. The sound effects were so impressive, though. Zac had his eyes tightly closed. 'Hey, are you all right?' I asked.

'Oh, yes,' he murmured and still with his eyes closed he went on, 'This is one part of the war I really wouldn't have liked. Did you know that in London during the Blitz they had fifty-seven continuous nights of bombing?'

Fifty-seven nights of horror and death screeching down on them. How did they stand it?

Outside our bombing went on and on. Once the whole house seemed to be picked up and shaken. Solly was cowering underneath Barney's pyjama

140

top.

'Are you scared too?' Solly asked me in a hoarse whisper.

'A bit,' I replied. 'Even though I do know it's not real.'

Solly tilted his head to one side. 'How much longer will this bombing last?'

'We don't know,' said Barney.

'I wasn't asking you,' said Solly. 'I'm asking my friend here.' And he gently snuggled his chin under my arm. I started to stroke him, just as if he were a nervous dog. 'How about if we sing some more songs,' said Solly. 'That might take our mind off the bombing.'

Farmer Benson thought Solly's idea was an excellent one. We'd just finished singing Underneath the Arches when the air-raid siren sounded again. Only this time it was the all clear.

Farmer Benson dashed outside to assess the damage, with us close behind. Several of the windows had been blown out and pieces of shrapnel littered the farmyard. Glass was scattered everywhere too. Farmer Benson looked as shocked as we did; I don't think he had believed that the television company would actually cause any damage. His face set, he rushed off to check on the animals again.

I looked at the glass and shivered. I just couldn't help it. But Leo whispered to me, 'Don't get too worked up.'

'I'm not,' I said.

'It isn't real, like I keep telling you— nothing is real in this place,' he said. 'They probably just threw all this stuff around.' He sounded angry. But I couldn't help thinking that Farmer Benson had looked pretty worried . . .

Then Leo told me about the warning he'd received at the evacuees' party.

'That's incredible,' I said. 'Was she trying to warn you about Harriet?'

'I haven't a single clue,' said Leo. 'But I can't stop thinking about it. I tell you, this is a dead weird place.'

'I had noticed.'

'Still, I'll be voted out tomorrow,' he said.

'No, you won't,' I replied. 'It'll be me for certain.'

'I hope you're not discussing tomorrow's eviction.' I hadn't noticed Harriet creep up beside us.

'We'd never do anything as shameful as that,' said Leo with a big grin on his face.

But when I got back to our bedroom a stern-faced Miss Weed was waiting for me. 'In the war,' she said, 'they had a saying—"Careless Talk Costs Lives". It can also get you evicted. You do not discuss who may or may not get evicted with anyone. Is that clear?'

'Yes, Miss Weed,' I said.

After Miss Weed had stalked out, I turned on Harriet. 'Did you tell her then?' I asked.

'No, I didn't,' she replied. 'You must have been observed talking about it on one of the cameras.'

I wasn't convinced, but I was just too tired to argue. And two minutes later (or that's what it felt like), Miss Weed came in clanging that awful bell again and telling us it was time to get up. I lay there for a few minutes, my head pounding with tiredness.

'You're going to be late,' chirped Harriet. 'And it's your turn to tidy up the room today—and you know how thorough Miss Weed's inspections are.'

'All right,' I said, dragging myself out of bed. Harriet was already dressed. 'This is sheer torture,' I murmured.

Harriet laughed. 'But it's all good, babe, isn't it?'

I put my hands over my ears. 'Harriet, don't say that so early in the morning. In fact, I may have to kill you if you ever say it again.'

Harriet laughed that deep, throaty, really irritating laugh. 'You are funny.'

'What do you mean?'

'Well, you go around moaning and hating everything. You don't seem to realize this is a unique experience for us.'

'Thanks for the lecture,' I grunted, and I sat on the bed. I had a hammering headache now. I think it was having to listen to Harriet's voice all the time. Then I realized Harriet was watching me. 'What are you looking at?' I asked.

'I've decided you're the funniest person I've ever met,' she said. Then she gave me one of her blinding smiles.

I picked up the jug of water and walked over to Harriet.

She went on grinning away.

'Here's something to really make you laugh,' I said.

And I tipped the jug of water all over Harriet's smug little face.

CHAPTER EIGHTEEN

Izzy in Trouble

Izzy

'Look what you've done,' gasped Harriet, her face deep red with shock.

And then she let out a scream which could have wiped out any number of air-raid sirens. In fact, it was so ear-piercingly, earth-shatteringly loud, I had to jump away from her.

Seconds later Miss Weed, Farmer Benson, Mrs Benson, Zac, Barney and Leo all charged into our bedroom. Then they just gaped at Harriet, who was looking all mournful and dripping water everywhere.

'Is this your doing?' demanded Miss

Weed of me.

'Well, yes, I'm afraid I sort of tripped over.'

'Don't be afraid,' murmured Leo, 'be proud.'

'Tell the truth at least,' wailed Harriet. 'You didn't trip at all, you did it deliberately. Admit it.'

'All right,' I said quietly, 'I admit it.'

'You, downstairs now,' said Miss Weed to me. 'I'm sure Mr Wallack will have something to say to you when he hears about this.'

I had no doubt he would. Harriet went downstairs too, escorted by Mrs Benson to dry off in the kitchen. The boys disappeared with Farmer Benson to do the outdoor tasks which are far too strenuous for mere girlies, while I stood in the hallway waiting for Mr Cheery Chuckles.

A few minutes later he arrived and after a whispered briefing from Miss Weed he barked, 'Follow me.' I stood in the sitting room, while he walked round me with this appalled look on his face as if I were some especially gruesome exhibit at the Chamber of Horrors.

'I'm beyond disappointed,' he said at last. 'And I'm trying to understand you.'

'Good luck with that,' I said, and I tried to smile.

His face grew even bleaker (if this was possible). 'Why on earth did you do it?' he asked.

'I really don't know,' I said.

'I've never a met a student with such a bad attitude as you.'

I hung my head. I did feel sort of ashamed. I mean, you really shouldn't go throwing jugs of water over people, no matter how insane they make you feel.

'I am now giving you a second warning,' said Wally. 'One more warning and you will be automatically evicted. Do you understand?'

'Totally,' I said.

I went upstairs. And I knew the word 'sorry' just had to leap out of my mouth. So straightaway I said, 'Harriet, I'm very, very sorry for tipping water over you.'

She was drying her hair. 'Are you really sorry?' she said. 'Or are you just pretending?'

'Oh, no, I'm very, very sorry.'

'And do you sincerely mean it?' she demanded.

'Yes,' I cried, a bit impatiently now.

'All right then.' She put down her towel and walked over to me. Then she gave me this big, sloppy hug. I nearly vomited with horror. 'I know you've got tons of problems and can't control yourself, so I shouldn't get mad at you. Instead, I'm going to try and help you.'

'Thanks,' I whispered.

'I so want to be your friend over the next few days.'

'Thanks,' I said again, in an even fainter voice.

Then she added sweetly, 'That's if you don't get voted out tonight, of course.'

CHAPTER NINETEEN

Eviction Night

Zac

That evening we all gathered round the kitchen table. Leo, Izzy and Barney sat together, their faces tense with nerves when they didn't think anyone was watching. And in the corner of the kitchen were their bags, all packed.

Solly Seal began shivering. 'Is he sickening for something?' asked Izzy.

'No,' Barney replied. 'It's just he really doesn't want to leave.'

Izzy rubbed his head. 'I think you'll be all right, Solly.'

Then Sig breezed in. We'd met him that first day at the studio. Now he was back in a bright blue blazer and waving an envelope about. 'Hello, folks,' he said. 'I have here the results of the viewers' votes. And they have been voting in their thousands for you.'

'They must be mad then,' said Leo.

But I saw he'd gone very still now. Izzy wasn't moving either.

Suddenly Barney whispered, 'Let us four join hands.' He was in the middle, so his hand clasped Leo's while Solly nuzzled against Izzy's hand. Mr Wallack noticed this and frowned, but he didn't say anything.

'Now, unhappily, the person with the least votes,' said Sig, his face suddenly sagging with sadness, 'must leave the Second World War for good. You will be escorted back to modern life . . .'

A grim, square-jawed woman in wartime uniform, who I'd never seen before, loomed into view.

'And in London you will meet up with your family again, who have been following your adventures,' went on Sig. 'So now, the moment of truth.' He ripped open the envelope. Then he said, 'Leo . . .'

Leo immediately jumped up. 'OK, I'm ready. Freedom, here I come. I'd like to say it's been fun—but really it hasn't. See you all in 2009, and keep it fresh, all right.'

'Leo,' cried Sig. 'If you'd let me

finish; I was about to tell you that you're safe—and will not be leaving this time.'

Leo couldn't stop a little smile flickering across his face. Neither could I. I hadn't liked him at all at first, but now I'd have really missed him.

'Are you sure I'm staying?' asked Leo.

'Positive,' said Sig.

'Then I demand a recount.'

'Leo, sit down,' hissed Mr Wallack.

Leo plonked himself down again and Sig turned to Izzy, Barney and Solly. 'It is between you two.'

'Three,' corrected Solly.

Sig smiled. 'What am I thinking of? Three. The first person to leave *Strictly Evacuees* is . . .'

CHAPTER TWENTY

The First Evictee Leaves

Izzy

Of course Sig made us wait about twenty thousand years before he announced the loser's name.

But finally, finally, a word escaped from his lips: 'Barney,' followed by, 'and Solly too, I'm afraid.'

I'd been holding my breath for so long that I started gasping frantically: a huge rush of relief, of course. But then I caught a glimpse of Barney's face. And just for a second there he looked absolutely shattered. All his dreams of TV fame had come crashing down on him.

And Solly just seemed to wilt in front of us. I patted him and said, 'I'm really sorry.' Yes, I spoke to Solly before Barney, how mad is that? But Solly looked so little and defeated—and all right, I know he isn't real, but I still felt dead sorry for him.

Then Sig announced, 'Barney and Solly, it's time for you to be whizzed back to the present. You have three minutes to leave your wartime home.'

Barney put on a big act then, grinning all over his face as if he'd just won the lottery. 'This is fantastic, as I'm now off to the land of Big Macs and computer games and twenty-four-hour telly, so I couldn't be happier.'

Harriet and I both gave Barney and Solly big hugs. Then, to my surprise, Leo and Zac did too. Leo looked quite sick with sadness, and I totally understood why.

I'd only known him and Barney and Zac for a few days, yet I felt closer to them—I felt closer to Solly, for goodness' sake—than to any of my friends back home. 'I'll miss you so much,' I whispered to Barney.

'Rebels United,' Solly whispered back.

Farmer and Mrs Benson looked pretty miserable as well—Mrs Benson in particular had loved Solly. I think they were very surprised too. Well, so was I, as I'd even thought Barney might win *this show.*

Then the song We'll Meet Again *started up. 'That means we must go,' said Sig, moving Barney and Solly towards the door where the woman in the Second World War uniform was waiting. She was holding both Barney's wartime bag and the one with all his 2009 stuff in.*

'And Barney,' I cried, 'it really doesn't end here. This is just the start of your dream.'

Barney struggled to say something, but then looked away. And in the end Solly had the last word. He cried, 'You're all winners—except for Mr Wallack.' We cheered that—and then Barney and Solly vanished into 2009.

'That was horrible,' I said to Leo.

'And how on earth are we still here?' he questioned. 'I felt sure it would be you or me. No offence,' he added.

'None taken,' I said, 'as I'd thought exactly the same.'

'Maybe,' he said, 'the public just like trouble-makers. In fact, that's probably why we're here in the first place. They want a few bolshy characters to shake

things up.'

I stared at him. 'I never understood why I was here before . . . but if you're right, then this programme is just a pantomime really.'

'And we're the Ugly Sisters,' grinned Leo.

Then Wally clapped his hands and said, 'Life will go on here as usual for the four remaining evacuees. But I do have one important announcement for you all. Tomorrow, one of you will be set a challenge. I won't tell you who it will be—or anything about the challenge—except that it will involve prompt action and quick thinking. If this individual is successful, they will earn extra rations for the whole group. So, good luck, and get ready for a challenge when you least expect it.'

'What exactly will this challenge involve?' I asked.

'I'm sorry, no more questions,' said Wally. 'In wartime, there was a strong element of surprise which demanded split-second responses—that is what we will be testing tomorrow. So, expect the unexpected.'

Then Leo asked, 'And when is our next jolly eviction?'

Wally said firmly, 'You will be told that information in due course. No more questions now.'

Everything was designed to keep us confused and on edge. I really hated that.

Then Miss Weed said, 'Leo and Isobel, you may go upstairs and unpack.'

To my horror, Harriet added, 'And I'll help you, Isobel.'

'That's very kind of you, Harriet,' said Miss Weed approvingly.

Upstairs, Harriet smiled sweetly at me. 'I'll help you put your things away tidily.'

Even when Harriet was being nice, she set my teeth on edge.

'No, you're all right,' I mumbled.

'Oh, don't be silly,' said Harriet. Then she pranced around the room, laughing that annoying, tinkling laugh as she ever so carefully put all my belongings away. 'You and I are going to have such a great time together, aren't we, babe?'

I didn't trust myself to answer. I just kept glancing longingly at the jug of water in the corner of the room.

CHAPTER TWENTY-ONE

Dramatic News

Zac

I was very tired and thought, I'll fall asleep as soon as my head hits the pillow tonight. I opened the bedroom door. 'I'm sorry Barney had to leave, but I was jolly pleased it wasn't—'

Then I stopped, because I'd noticed something extremely odd. The wardrobe door was open and Leo was crouched down with his head right inside it, while his manner was highly furtive and anxious.

I stared at him in amazement.

Then he motioned me to join him.

What was he up to now? Was this one of his silly jokes? But I'd never seen him look more serious.

'What on earth are you doing?' I asked.

He put a finger to his lips. Then he said, very very quietly, 'I've found out who snitched on me.'

CHAPTER TWENTY-TWO

Who Can You Trust?

Zac

'Who?' I gasped.

Leo mouthed at me to be quiet; then with his head still deep in the wardrobe whispered: 'Someone in this room.'

'No—' I began indignantly.

'Oh, I don't mean you,' he whispered. 'I mean the other person in here.'

Then I thought he must have gone mad. The stress had obviously got to him. But Leo motioned me to follow him and started making 'Be quiet' signals. He got up and very slowly moved the picture on the wall. He pointed. I looked, and then jumped back in amazement. There were wires behind there and a small microphone.

I couldn't believe it.

I struggled to speak. But Leo signalled me to return to the wardrobe. Once inside there I whispered, 'This room's bugged.'

'Of course it is,' said Leo. 'I'm annoyed with myself for not spotting it before. But tonight I had a buzzy think and found it almost at once.'

'But they said . . .' I began.

'They said there weren't any cameras, which is sort of true. But they didn't mention there's a secret microphone in here,' said Leo.

'You know,' I cried suddenly, 'I think that's what that woman was trying to warn you about yesterday.'

'Of course it was.' Leo lowered his voice. 'So conversations we thought were secret are actually being broadcast to the world.'

'But why would they do that?' I cried. 'Do you suppose it's to check we're all right?'

'Don't be stupid,' said Leo. 'It's to mess with our heads.'

159

'Oh, no,' I cried.

'Oh, yes,' he replied. 'They let us think one of the evacuees has snitched on us, believing that will totally stir things up. And that's what they really want—trouble.'

I opened my mouth to argue—but I couldn't.

Leo swept on. 'Of course, all the adults are in on it.'

'Not Farmer Benson,' I piped up at once.

'No, he's got to be in on it,' said Leo. 'I mean, it's his house and they'd have to get his permission to plant bugs everywhere.'

I shook my head firmly. 'You were wrong about Harriet being a spy—and you're definitely wrong about him.'

'No, I'm not. I always thought he was a bit too good to be true. That's his cover, getting us to trust him.'

'No,' I shouted. 'Not him.'

'Keep your voice down,' hissed Leo. 'What's the matter with you?'

'You don't understand,' I said, still worked up. 'I don't care about winning this show. I mean, I want to stay here

160

until the end, of course, but I'd be so happy if you won it. And that's the truth. You see I'm here for quite a different reason. Well, actually, I've got a secret.'

Leo's eyes widened. 'What's that then?'

'I'm going to live here on this farm until I'm grown up—just like Victor did.'

'Says who?' demanded Leo.

'Well, just me at the moment. But Farmer Benson said he doesn't know how he'll manage without me and Mrs Benson likes the way I always clear my plate. So I know I'll fit in here just fine.'

Leo shook his head.

'What?' I asked.

'I thought *I* was crazy.' He shook his head again. 'But you—you've just decided you're going to live here for good?'

'Well, until I'm eighteen, yes.'

'What about your family? Won't they look round one day and say, "Where's that funny little guy who used to live here? What was his name now? Zac,

161

that's it. We haven't seen him for a few months."'

'Well, you know my mum's dead.'

Leo actually blushed. 'Izzy did say something, but I'd sort of forgotten. Sorry.'

'That's all right,' I said. And then I quickly told him the whole story. 'And so you see,' I concluded, 'me moving here really is the ideal solution.'

Leo considered this and then said slowly, 'So it's very important to you that Farmer Benson is on the level.'

'Very, very important,' I said.

'Well, let's find out, shall we?'

I looked at him in some alarm. He seemed all fired up as if suddenly he could do anything. 'What are you going to do?'

'Ask him,' said Leo.

Before I could say another word, Leo had already stormed out of the wardrobe, opened the front door and yelled: 'To whom it may concern; I need to perform Number Two, and with some urgency as well.'

A door opened almost at once and Miss Weed hissed up the stairs,

'There's no need to shout.'

'Sorry, but I'm desperate,' said Leo.

Then Miss Weed was at our door. 'It would be appreciated if one night you didn't have to disturb the whole house,' she said. 'But I'll see if Farmer Benson is available. Do you need to use the facilities as well, Zac?'

'I really do,' I said.

'Well, please wait very quietly.'

After she'd disappeared Leo and I had another quick meeting—in the wardrobe. Leo murmured, 'On the way to the loo, I shall ever so casually ask Farmer Benson if he knew our bedroom was bugged. I shall continue to cross-examine him, and if he jumps in an alarmed fashion or does anything remotely shifty I'll spot it right away.' Then he added, 'And don't be too upset if he's guilty—you can always come and live with me. We've got a spare bed and everything.'

'Thank you, but it won't be necessary,' I said firmly. But inside, my stomach was twisting about. I had total confidence in Farmer Benson, but I was also apprehensive, and even a bit scared.

Downstairs Farmer Benson said brightly, 'It's the same drill as before, lads, and I expect you know the way blindfolded by now, don't you?' We stumbled along with Farmer Benson saying conversationally, 'Let's hope we don't have the air-raid siren going off again tonight.'

As we reached the loo, Leo said softly, 'No cameras here, are there?'

'No, the lavatory is out of bounds,' said Farmer Benson.

Leo had a quick look round at the outside of the loo. 'I think we're safe here,' he concluded.

'Safe?' echoed Farmer Benson.

'Yeah, the thing is, Zac and I made a terrible discovery tonight. Found out our bedroom was bugged.'

Farmer Benson turned sharply. 'What do you mean?'

Leo explained quickly and breathlessly, all the time staring accusingly at Farmer Benson. Then he asked, 'So did you know anything about that?'

'I assure you lads,' Farmer Benson

said, 'that I knew nothing.'

'Are you sure?' demanded Leo. 'It's your house.'

'Yes, but don't forget we went to a hotel for a week while they installed all the cameras. I turned up once and it was so noisy it sounded as if they were knocking the farm down. They wouldn't even let me inside. I'd taken the disruption fee—and this meant what they did was none of my business. But I'm very shocked at what you've just told me.'

Leo gave me a quick nod. I knew exactly what that meant: he believed Farmer Benson.

My heart just swelled with relief then, even though I'd always been certain Farmer Benson couldn't be a part of any secret bugging.

'We don't know half of what's going on here,' went on Farmer Benson. 'Well, they only told us about that air raid at the very last moment. And'—he lowered his voice—'to be honest, this is an odder show than we were expecting. All that noise the other night, for instance. We thought . . . well, I certainly never expected there'd be secret microphones in the bedrooms. I suppose I ought to check our room now.' He gave a rather mirthless chuckle.

'I just hope,' said Leo, 'this conversation with you isn't being bugged somehow.'

Farmer Benson looked around. 'I really don't see how it could be.'

'Unless there are secret bugs in the paper holder in there,' I said, nodding at the toilet.

Then Farmer Benson said, 'So do you want me to have a word . . . ?'

'No,' almost shouted Leo. 'Knowledge is power, as they say, so I don't want them to realize I'm on to them yet. Then, when they're least expecting it I'll strike.'

He said this with worrying eagerness; that's why I added quickly, 'But we don't want to let one thing ruin the rest of the evacuation experience, because it might not be anything sinister. It could just be . . . well, in 2009 there are cameras and bugging devices everywhere. And people have very

166

good reasons for doing that.'

Leo raised two highly sceptical eyebrows.

'And apart from the bugging,' I continued, 'these past few days have been the most magnificent and brilliant and memorable of my entire life . . . and you just wait until Wednesday, when Victor returns—to the very farm he grew up on—for the first time in over sixty years.'

'That should be a great moment,' agreed Farmer Benson.

But later Leo summoned me to the wardrobe once more. 'I've just made a decision.'

'What's that then?'

'Tomorrow afternoon, after we've done our chores and just before the meal, I shall face Wally with my discovery.' He grinned all over his face. 'Don't you love it when you've got something on adults, especially the really mean ones, like Wally? You just watch him crumble tomorrow.'

CHAPTER TWENTY-THREE

The Challenge

Zac

Next day began with Leo jumping out of bed and yelling, 'Had another dream about Miss Weed last night; must have been the sight of her in her lovely dressing gown. Cor!!' Then he fell about laughing. Later, he whispered to me excitedly, 'Just wait until I expose them tonight.'

But I was worried Leo might get carried away and say something he shouldn't. And I really didn't want him to be up for eviction again.

I thought there would be a chance to warn him to be careful when we were doing our chores. But today only Leo was working on the farm, while Harriet and Izzy went off with Mrs Benson to deliver some cakes to the old people's home. I was given another task: to collect some food from the local village shop.

I walked past the security man on the gate. I had to show him a letter written by Miss Weed saying I had permission to go out. I thought it was a shame the security man wasn't in wartime costume. A cameraman was some way in front of me, but I'd learned now to totally ignore him and I enjoyed strolling through the village.

Then I passed a man whose Second World War clothes I recognized instantly. 'Settling in all right at the farm?' he asked. He had one of those pencil-thin moustaches so popular in the 1940s. I grinned at him. I was allowed to converse with people who were in costume.

'Yes, thank you very much. Everyone's extremely friendly.'

He nodded and went off. I wondered vaguely if he was an actor or one of the locals dressed up.

The shop was a modern one, but the lady behind the counter was again in old-fashioned clothes. She greeted me, 'Ah, you must be one of the evacuees.'

I smiled politely and said, 'Yes,

169

ma'am, I am.'

'Well, I've got your order ready. Are you sure you can carry it all?'

'Oh, yes,' I assured her. 'I'm much stronger than I look.'

Actually, the bag was quite heavy, but I whistled *Run, Rabbit, Run* as I stumbled along. Just as I was turning into my home (and that's exactly how I saw it now), a man on a bike came speeding towards me. I recognized his uniform instantly. He was from the Home Guard. I was thrilled to see him. He got off his bike. He was a very big, bulky man.

'Here, lad,' he said calling me over. 'We've had a tip-off, some enemy agents have landed.'

I gave a shiver of anticipation. Here it was. The challenge Mr Wallack had mentioned. I'd been so busy worrying about Leo's discovery I'd forgotten all about that. But it looked as if I'd been chosen. And I did so want to win extra rations for everyone.

'Do you want me to help search for enemy agents?' I asked eagerly.

The man smiled. 'No, no . . . we'll do

that. It's maps of the area we need urgently. Can you get us some now?'

'Yes, of course,' I cried, hastily trying to remember where the maps were kept. Ah yes, now I remembered—inside the second drawer of the bureau in the living room. By a lucky coincidence, Farmer Benson had been showing them to me only two nights ago. 'Just one thing,' I added. 'Have you got any identification on you at all?'

I thought he might be cross at me asking. But he said, 'Well done, lad.' His ID card flashed in front of me.

'Thank you very much for letting me view that,' I said.

'Now will you hurry,' urged the man, 'as we're very short of time.'

'I'll be faster than the wind.' Then I added, 'Would you mind just looking after my bag for me? I'll run much faster if I'm not carrying that.' The man nodded and smiled. And I jetted off down the track.

I tore inside the farm. For the first time since I'd arrived, the house was completely empty. It felt different without anyone in it, much bigger and more watchful somehow. As if the house itself was waiting to see if I could find those maps.

And I did, almost right away. My hand shook slightly as I gathered them up; best to let him have every one. It was for the war effort.

Then I raced out again. The Home Guard looked at his watch as I sprang towards him. I think he might have been timing me. 'There you are,' I said. 'Every map of the area I could find. Was I fast enough?' I added anxiously.

'Very fast, I'm impressed, and these will prove extremely useful.' He got on his bike again. 'For now, don't tell anyone about this.'

'As careless talk costs lives,' I said.

He nodded approvingly. 'Quite right.'

Then he rode off, once more finding time to give me a quick wave as he did so.

That was such a gratifying moment. And I felt so pleased with myself—but not in a big-headed way, just very relieved I hadn't messed up. Then I took the shopping inside and shortly afterwards people came back again. I wondered if they'd been kept away deliberately as part of my test.

I longed to tell someone what I'd done, but I remembered how the Home Guard officer had impressed on me the importance of keeping quiet about it.

Then Mr Wallack ordered us into the kitchen for what he called a de-briefing.

'Hope this won't take long,' said Izzy to me. 'I'm starving . . .' Then she asked, 'What are you looking so happy about?'

'I wasn't aware that I was,' I said.

'Oh, yes,' said Izzy. 'You can't stop grinning, neither can Leo. What's going on?'

Of course, Leo and I were smiling about quite different things. Leo said to Izzy, 'All will be revealed very shortly.'

Before I could reply Mr Wallack had strode into the kitchen and was asking for silence. He always expected to be obeyed instantly. He was joined at the

173

front by Miss Weed. Farmer Benson and Mrs Benson also came in and sat at the back.

'I've summoned you all here—' began Mr Wallack.

But then Leo jumped to his feet. 'Actually, I've got an important announcement to make first,' he said.

Mr Wallack's face twitched furiously. 'How dare you interrupt me like that! How *dare* you. One more word from you and you will receive a warning.'

He looked so angry that Leo just muttered, 'You just wait, mate,' and sat down.

'Now,' continued Mr Wallack, 'before I was so rudely interrupted, I mentioned to you yesterday that one of you would be set a challenge. That challenge was performed this afternoon.'

There was a murmur of surprise, while a modest little smile began playing about my lips.

'One of you was stopped by this person.' And right on cue the Home Guard man strode in. 'He is, of course,' said Mr Wallack, 'in a Home Guard uniform and he asked one of you for maps as he claimed he needed them to track down spies.'

The way Mr Wallack said 'claimed' sent a horrible shudder rushing down my spine. Then he asked the Home Guard soldier to speak. In a grave 'War has been declared' voice, the man said, 'I stole this Home Guard uniform. I am in fact a fifth columnist—a spy. I needed maps for the invaders. And the boy I asked just handed the maps over. Didn't you, Zac?'

He saw the deep horror on my face and gave a little smile of triumph. 'But,' I cried out suddenly, 'I asked for your ID card.'

'Yes,' he agreed, 'you did, but you didn't look at the card carefully enough.' He produced the card again. 'First of all, my date of birth is 1917, but look how I've done the seven with the line across the middle of it. Not a British style at all in those days.'

'How could he be expected to know that?' cried Leo.

'All right, but surely he should have

spotted the card wasn't signed.' The man waved the ID card about so that everyone could see it and then he turned to me. 'Shouldn't you have spotted that, Zac?'

I couldn't even speak now. I just gave my head a stiff little shake.

'By his actions today,' continued the Home Guard, 'Zac has given the enemy immense help.'

Shocked, ashamed, I couldn't stop the tears from trickling down my face. 'I'm very sorry,' I croaked.

'So no extra rations for us,' called out Izzy. 'Oh well, it's no big deal.'

'I'm afraid it is,' said Mr Wallack. 'Zac, stand up, please.'

I stumbled to my feet.

'With great regret, Zac, your journey is now over.'

'What . . . ?' I faltered.

'You are being evicted from the wartime house immediately.'

There were shocked cries of disbelief from everyone around me. Even Farmer and Mrs Benson looked stunned. And I . . . I just couldn't take it in. I stood there, blood pounding in my ears, sick with shock.

I'd been banished from my new home. So this meant I'd have to return to Aunt Sara's and go back to being weird little Zac, the nuisance, who never fitted in and never would.

No, I couldn't go back there. Ever.

What else could I do? I stood there, totally and completely lost. I had to try and speak, so I asked, shakily, 'At least let me stay until . . .' Only I couldn't even finish my sentence as this giant hand had started shaking me, or that's exactly what it felt like—and now the whole room was spinning faster and faster . . .

CHAPTER TWENTY-FOUR

'I'm Staying Here'

Izzy

I made a little noise in my throat like a startled turkey. Zac evicted from the house—because he hadn't checked an ID card was signed? It was a mad joke. It had to be.

Then Zac began swaying about as if he was going to faint. Leo, Harriet and I all jumped up, but Zac gripped the back of his chair tightly and said, 'No, I'm all right, honestly.' He stood there, sweat crawling down his face and then cried, 'Please let me stay here. I realize I have lost the competition. I really never cared about that anyway. But may I stay at least until tomorrow—because Victor . . .'

'I'm very sorry,' murmured Wally, 'but you must leave at once.'

'I'll do any number of extra tasks,' Zac persisted, 'and you needn't even feed me. But don't make me go back now.'

Zac was practically begging now. No, he was begging. And I hated seeing that. So I called out, 'Excuse me, but you never said if you messed up the challenge, you'd be chucked out.'

'No,' said Wally, 'but we did tell you to expect the unexpected, didn't we?' He turned to Miss Weed.

'Yes, that's right,' she agreed, although not very loudly.

'Give him another challenge tomorrow then,' said Leo.

'Yes, please do that,' I urged as politely as I could.

Wally didn't answer for a few seconds and just when a faint hope was rising in me he said, 'Team spirit is admirable. I like team spirit—but here it is wholly misplaced. A decision has been made and it is final. Already a new boy has been selected for the competition and he will be joining us for breakfast tomorrow.'

'That's not fair,' I murmured.

'And if anyone objects, then they too can join Zac in leaving right now. We have a waiting list with several hundred other names on it, desperate for their chance. Now, has anyone else anything to say?'

I had plenty, but I really didn't want to be thrown out. So I just lowered my head. So did Leo.

Then a brief, supercharged silence before Wally said smoothly, 'Now, Zac, will you go and pack. You are supposed to leave in five minutes, but I will give you an additional ten minutes. All right?'

Zac didn't reply. He just stood there, staring at the wall opposite. In the end I got up and went over to him. 'Zac,' I said very softly. He didn't react; I don't think he even heard me. He just went on gazing at the wall, his eyes not even blinking.

I wondered if Zac was ever going to talk to anyone again. That sounds such a crazy thing to write now, but you didn't see Zac's eyes then; they looked as if he'd been hypnotised.

'He's very, very shocked,' I said. 'Could you give—' I began.

'Zac, leave now,' ordered Wally, his

180

voice as cold as steel. Zac still didn't react. Miss Weed and Wally looked at each other.

'Poor lad,' said Farmer Benson from the back of the room, 'it's been a huge shock for him.'

Mrs Benson made agreeing noises and then asked, 'Shall I give him a hand?'

But at that moment Zac got to his feet. Only he looked so weird, like someone in a trance. He said: 'I shall go upstairs, but I'm afraid I will not be packing. I do apologize for any inconvenience my decision may cause.'

Then he moved towards the stairs like a sleepwalker. His tone had been so polite, yet what he'd said was dynamite. He was going to totally disobey Wally's instructions. Leo and I might talk big— but here was the true rebel.

I watched him trail up the stairs with a mixture of shock and admiration.

'I think I should help him pack,' said Miss Weed.

'No, it's all right,' cried out Harriet unexpectedly, 'I'll do that.'

I shot her a look of utter hatred. How could she volunteer to do that? She really was the most loathsome girl I'd ever met. And she didn't have one atom of loyalty towards her fellow evacuees. Not even for Zac, who always spoke up for her. Well, I didn't care how much trouble I got into—I was tipping another jug of water over her tonight, for sure.

'Actually,' said Wally, 'I think it might be best if Harriet does assist Zac.'

'Yes, yes,' agreed Miss Weed at once. I don't think she wanted to force Zac to leave. But, of course, Harriet had no such scruples and she smirked proudly at the teachers before she glided upstairs.

'Well, now I shall leave you with Miss Weed,' said Wally, 'but I shall be back with some important announcements about tomorrow later. You two,' he said, nodding at Leo and me, 'can start laying the table for tea.'

'Do we set a place for Zac?' asked Leo.

'No, of course you don't,' said Wally, flushing angrily.

He strode off and I turned to Miss Weed. 'Zac should not have to leave. You can't do this to him.'

For a moment I thought Miss Weed

was going to agree with me. She definitely hesitated. But then she clapped her hands as if Leo and I were disobedient puppies. 'Come on, you have work to do—no more backchat.'

As Leo and I started bunging out the cutlery and place mats, Leo murmured, 'On the bright side, Zac hasn't ever got to see Wally or Miss Weed again.' But that didn't make me feel one millimetre better. Somehow I felt we'd really let Zac down, leaving him to the tender mercies of Harriet.

Then Farmer and Mrs Benson strode into the kitchen and beckoned to Miss Weed. 'May we have a word with you?' the farmer asked.

'Yes, of course,' she said, not exactly eagerly. Then she turned to us. 'Now carry on, you two,' she said, before joining Farmer and Mrs Benson outside the kitchen door.

Of course Leo and I immediately started ear-wigging.

Farmer Benson was speaking very quietly at first, so it was hard to catch a single word, but then we heard him say, 'We thought this was going to be a social experiment, that's why we agreed to let our farm to be used. But what you did tonight—'

And his wife interrupted, 'I feel ashamed to be a part of it. You're just playing with children's emotions and now you've got a boy upstairs breaking his heart.'

Miss Weed whispered something very faintly and the next sound we heard was the back door being pushed open. And we realized they were carrying on this conversation in the farmyard.

Good old Bensons standing up for Zac. But they also made me feel even more ashamed. 'We shouldn't have left Zac up there with Harriet.' I spat out her name.

'No, we shouldn't,' said Leo. Then he hesitated. We both did.

'So,' I said, 'are we going to slip up and see him now?'

Leo didn't answer. He just started going upstairs.

I sped after him.

And then I got a shock.

Harriet wasn't with Zac at all. No, she was in our room. I marched in, closely *followed by Leo.*

And then I got a gigantic shock.

Harriet was packing.

CHAPTER TWENTY-FIVE

Harriet's Secret

Izzy

'What are you doing?' I stuttered.

'It looks remarkably like she's packing to me,' muttered Leo.

'Score one hundred points for observation. Yes, I'm leaving instead of Zac,' said Harriet.

'Says who?' I asked.

'Says me,' she said.

'But why would you do that?' asked Leo

'Before I answer,' said Harriet, 'I'd better warn you, this room is bugged.'

'So's ours,' said Leo. 'I meant to tell you all tonight.'

'Oh, don't worry,' cried Harriet. 'I've known the room was bugged since day

185

one, and anything we say in here can—and probably will—be broadcast.'

I looked at her in total amazement. She seemed completely different suddenly. And her wet, annoying smile had just vanished.

She saw me staring at her and smiled. 'You never guessed, did you, Izzy? I was sure you would.' Before I could reply she was off bustling round the room again. 'Well, I shan't be sorry to lose that wretched gas mask. I don't know how people put up with them for six years, do you?'

I didn't answer. I was still reeling from what she'd just said. 'What do you mean I never guessed?' I said at last. And then as I stared at her again, I added, 'You seem like a totally different person suddenly.'

'That's a relief,' she said briskly. 'I don't know how much longer I could have gone on saying "It's all good, babe" and doing that awful simpering smile.'

I gaped at her. 'Have you . . .' I said slowly, 'just been pretending to be annoying?'

'Of course I have,' she said.

Leo, who'd been watching all this intently while squatting on the end of my bed, said, 'Sorry, but this is really weirding me out, Harriet. Why would you pretend to be annoying?'

'The truth is,' said Harriet, 'I'm an actress—well, a wannabe actress, who's never had the whisper of a part on TV before. I've been going to auditions since I was six. I'm seventeen, by the way.'

'No way,' I yelled.

Leo shook his head in an amazed sort of way too.

'And I had to get through three auditions for this part actually.'

'This part . . .' Leo repeated.

'Oh, yes,' grinned Harriet with an impish grin I'd never seen before. 'On the first night they let the viewers know I was really a seventeen-year-old actress, on a secret mission. That was the show's secret challenge. Would you sniff out that I wasn't a genuine thirteen-year-old? If none of you guessed my secret identity, I got a part for at least six episodes in a TV soap.'

'You should still get that,' said Leo.

'Because you fooled us completely,' I added.

'Somehow,' said Harriet, 'I don't think they'll be giving me any pats on the back tonight.' Then she faced us. 'Now my other secret challenge, as they put it, was to really irritate you, Izzy. I had to be the person you'd least like to share a room with: your nightmare.'

'But why?' I asked.

'So you'd lose your temper,' said Leo.

'Exactly,' said Harriet.

'The madder I got you, the better they liked it; makes for great telly and all that. So when you threw that jug of water over me I was thrilled.' She walked over and faced me. 'In fact, I was amazed you hadn't done it a lot sooner.' She went on, 'When I first met you, Izzy, I liked you a lot. And I thought, can I really wind up this poor girl day after day? And for a few minutes I wanted out. Remember on the train when I rushed off, saying I was sick?'

Leo and I nodded.

'I told them I couldn't go through with it. But Wally gave me this big lecture, said this was my big chance and I might never get another. So I gave in.' She looked at me. 'No hard feelings?'

'None at all,' I replied. Then I added, 'But now you've given it all up.'

Harriet turned away. 'Yeah, well I saw the way they treated poor Zac tonight. And why? To create another sensation, to get viewers talking. No thanks. Not for me. Hadn't one of you better check he's all right, by the way?'

'I'll go,' I said.

Zac was just sitting on his bed, staring into space.

And before I could say anything, Wally's voice erupted out of nowhere. 'I want everyone downstairs. You will all go to the classroom immediately.' His voice seemed to fill the whole room.

And suddenly Zac came out of his trance. 'He sounds very angry,' he whispered.

'Do you think so?' I said. 'He just sounded his usual miserable self to me. Still, I suppose we'd better go down.'

But I was far more anxious than I sounded. As I hadn't a clue what was going to happen next.

Not a clue.

CHAPTER TWENTY-SIX

Who Leaves?

Izzy

The heavy gloom of our classroom was bad enough in the daylight. At night it was even worse. Especially as there was just one dim light flickering away in this shadowy chamber of doom.

A wave of fear rushed over me.

'Hey, this is scary,' whispered Leo to me. 'Do you suppose Miss Weed will give me a cuddle to cheer me up?'

'Ask her if you like,' I grinned.

'No talking,' snapped Miss Weed. She stood at the front of the classroom, as still as a bookend. I grinned at Harriet. She gave me a triumphant wave, and she looked very relaxed. Perhaps it was a

relief to be herself at last.

Would she be evicted now? I didn't want her to be. (And I never thought I'd want Harriet to stay.) But if she was chucked out, did that mean Zac was now safe? Poor Zac, he just looked totally confused.

'Class will rise.' I hadn't heard Wally come in and his voice made me jump. He strode to the front of the room, frowning heavily. He brought a sharp coldness with him. In fact, this room was suddenly freezing. His unblinking eyes scanned the room sternly.

'There has been some highly unfortunate behaviour tonight,' he said at last. He looked at Harriet. 'I believe your cover has been broken.'

'Not by us though,' I called out. 'Harriet totally fooled everyone, including me.'

Wally did his impression of someone sucking a really sour sweet and then said to me, 'When will you learn you are back in wartime Britain where children only speak when they are spoken to?' He continued, 'Your cover has been blown, Harriet, so now you must be evicted.'

And at a signal from him the door opened and that woman in the Second World War uniform suddenly appeared again. 'Security will escort you away. Goodbye, Harriet.'

Harriet gazed round at the woman waiting for her and then turned to Wally. 'I hope Zac can stay now.' He didn't answer. Indeed, he seemed to be acting as if she'd already left. Harriet got to her feet and shrugged her shoulders. 'So that's it, I'm out of here.' She nodded at the woman. 'It's all right, I'll come quietly. You won't need any tranquillizer darts. Best of luck, everyone.'

We all called out to Harriet 'See you soon' and 'Good luck.' And then she was gone. I remember watching a pantomime once where this character suddenly disappeared down a trap door. It really horrified me. And now I felt as if that's what had just happened to Harriet.

Leo raised his hand.

'Yes, what is it?' snapped Wally.

'Excuse me raising this question with you, your great eminence,' said Leo, 'but I'd just like to know why you very

sneakily have been bugging our rooms?'

I thought Wally might really be angered by this question and Leo's sarky tone, but strangely he didn't seem to be. Instead he said smoothly, 'Because we wanted to get something completely natural and capture some very honest moments. This we have certainly achieved, and we believe the results justify our very minor subterfuge.' Before any of us could reply he went on, his voice absolutely brimming with authority now. 'Tomorrow, one new person will be joining Strictly Evacuees. There may well be others. For now, I am trusting you two'—he nodded at Leo and me—'to go straight back to the farm and have your tea. I will join you there shortly and tell you about tomorrow's very special group challenge. For now, though, you are dismissed.'

'What about Zac?' called out Leo.

'I'll be all right,' whispered Zac. 'You go.'

'Zac is not your concern,' snapped Wally. 'Leave him to Miss Weed and me.' As Wally said this he glanced across at her. Normally Miss Weed

193

gazed up adoringly at him as he spoke. But today she was standing very still and looking straight ahead. Then Wally went on in quite a gentle voice (for him), 'I shouldn't tell you this, but I will. The viewers' response to both of you has been extremely strong. And, in fact, you two have an extremely good chance . . . well, I wouldn't be surprised if either of you won this show.'

I stared at him in stunned disbelief, and then burst out, 'You're joking.'

To my great surprise Wally's mouth started twitching about. And he wasn't having a stroke. No, he was trying to smile. I had a feeling cheeriness didn't come very easily to him.

'No, you really could win this show, Isobel,' he said, still in a kindly tone. 'Or you, Leo. I just thought you'd like to know that.' He was struggling to smile again now, while the shock of what he'd just said exploded inside me.

I REALLY COULD WIN THIS SHOW.

Well, if I did—that would be the greatest moment of my life, without question. And right then I started picturing it: me stepping out of the farm; no doubt there'd be fireworks exploding everywhere and people cheering and waving banners with my name on.

And then Mum would rush up to me, looking so proud and happy. And I'd hand her the tickets for our holiday in the sun—maybe they'd be in a gold envelope. Yeah, I bet they would be. I'd give Mum the gold envelope and tell her that the good times were coming our way at last. This was the start of a total change in our fortunes now. And soon we'd be sun-tanned and rich and famous and . . .

I tell you, I was so busy picturing it all, I have no memory of leaving the classroom at all. I must have just floated out of it. The next thing I actually do remember is me walking back to the farm with Leo. And even then I didn't say anything. I couldn't, I was still so dazed and entranced by me winning Strictly Evacuees.

And then Leo stopped walking. 'Hey, what just happened in there?'

'What?' I murmured, slowly and reluctantly coming back to earth.

'I mean, did we just walk out of there without a word?' he asked.

'We must have.'

'So did old Wally put a spell on us with his weird eyes?'

'He said six magic words,' I replied. 'You really could win this show. *You started imagining it too, didn't you?*'

'For a few wacky seconds, yeah,' said Leo. He sounded ashamed. 'But we still don't know what's going to happen to Zac. We just abandoned him: our mate.' He stared at me. 'I think we should go back.'

I looked away.

'You think we should stroll off and leave him?' he persisted.

'No, no, no . . . well, yes.' Then I half whispered. 'This could be our time.'

'Yes, it could,' mocked Leo. 'Oh, this is our time to be famous. Wow and wow again.'

'You can laugh, but I absolutely hate not having any money . . . and my mum's really struggling . . .'

'So you're winning this show for your dear old mum,' cried Leo.

'Partly, yes.'

He smiled. 'I really do believe you.'

'But I am.'

'First of all,' he said, 'when Wally tells us we might win this show, smiling like a snake as he does so, do we believe him? Or do we think it's yet another of his little tricks?' Without waiting for me to answer he went on, 'And secondly, OK, you win. But this show is pretty much nuts. So you won't even be famous for fifteen minutes—more like fifteen seconds, if you're lucky. Still, the bad times you've had mean you're entitled to be famous. That's the deal, isn't it?'

'All right, Leo,' I said tightly.

'No, keep going, as you'll probably win a holiday. Not even Strictly Evacuees could lie about that. So, go back to the farmhouse. I might even vote for you myself.'

I heard myself swallow hard.

'Go on, I'll look out for Zac. It doesn't need two of us.'

Without another word I ran all the way to the farmhouse. And I know exactly what you're thinking: that girl is so wrapped up in herself, she'd even dump her mates just to win a show. I know, because it's exactly what I was thinking too.

I carried on going until I reached the door of the farmhouse. And then I stopped. It was as if I'd hit some invisible force field which was preventing me moving any further. I suppose you could say that my conscience finally stirred into action.

And after that my legs could only move one way: back to Leo. I called out his name in a funny, ragged voice I hardly recognized as belonging to me.

He whirled round.

'Wait for me,' I croaked.

CHAPTER TWENTY-SEVEN

A Shock Announcement

Izzy

Leo and I tore back into that classroom. It seemed even darker than before.

'What is the meaning of this?' demanded Wally, his face stiff with shock. 'You were told to return immediately to the farmhouse.'

Our bravery melted away just a bit then. And we both shuffled back a few steps. Then I noticed that Zac was standing up. He looked like a prisoner waiting to be sentenced. 'We just wondered,' I said, 'if Zac was staying on.'

'That's no business of yours,' said Wally and I didn't think he was going to say anything else. But then he went on very quietly, 'Zac will be leaving the farmhouse now, but he may be returning tomorrow. It is up to the

public to decide. If enough viewers call up and support him he'll be allowed back—won't you, Zac?'

Zac nodded slowly. He looked tired and very confused and that's exactly how Strictly Evacuees wanted it, of course. No doubt, at this very moment, thousands of people were going, 'Aaah, poor lad' and then stampeding to their phones to save Zac—while also making Strictly Evacuees tons and tons of dosh.

'Couldn't Zac wait for the viewers' verdict here with us?' asked Leo,

And then, quite unexpectedly, Miss Weed, who'd been standing very still beside Wally came to life. 'Actually, that might work, mightn't it?' she said brightly, hopefully. And I realized she really didn't want Zac to have to go away either.

But Wally shot her such a furious glare and snapped, 'I have already decided this. Zac must wait for the viewers' vote away from the farmhouse.'

Of course he must, I thought. That's much nastier for Zac—and so will get far more viewers ringing up.

Suddenly I felt very wise, very disillusioned—and very, very angry. This just isn't right, I thought. And then to my surprise I realized I'd said that aloud: 'This just isn't right.' *More words burst out of me then, my voice crackling with fury.* 'This isn't a show about time travel at all. No, it's a mad, roller-coaster ride where you play horrible mind games with us every second of the day; like secretly bugging our rooms, and bringing in actors to deliberately annoy us and putting Zac through—'

'Enough,' *roared Wally.* 'Leave the classroom now—or you will receive a third warning and be evicted.'

'I don't care,' *I cried, my face burning with anger.* 'I'm not leaving until Zac goes back to the farmhouse.' *And I sat down in a real I-shall-not-be-moved way. Then I looked at Leo, who'd been watching me, open-mouthed.*

'I'd like to agree with everything my esteemed evacuee has just said,' *he stated.* 'With great big brass knobs on. And just add that this whole show stinks worse than a Christmas dinner fart.'

For a few seconds after that it was so quiet you could have heard a snail cough. I think they call it dead air, on the radio. And it's not supposed to be very good.

But Wally just went on gaping at us, his eyes bulging in a confused sort of way. It was as if we'd started babbling away in a language he didn't understand. He really hadn't expected that outburst at all. And he was stuck now. He really was. His moustache kept rising and falling, as if it was being moved by a tiny invisible string. And there was a mad gleam in his eye, showing he'd slipped over completely to the crazed side. Anything could happen now.

He got up suddenly and slammed across the room towards Leo and me like a mad bull. What he was about to do to us we'll never know, because he was in such a state he tripped over his gown, didn't he?

He went on to perform one of the finest backward flips I've ever seen. He soared right up into the air and then landed with a mighty thud against the bookcase. Ancient books shot into the air and started dive-bombing Wally in a mad aggressive way, as if they too were disgusted with him, while a heavy trail of dust began to settle onto him too: he looked as if he was being covered in very elderly snow.

And it all happened so fast I couldn't even laugh, not then anyway. Miss Weed tore over to him, but he brushed her offer of help aside. He stumbled to his feet, furiously shaking his gown, his face grey with shock and fury.

Then the door suddenly burst open. And there was Farmer Benson—with Harriet. But she was supposed to have left ages ago. What was going on now?

'I've just been talking to this young lady,' said Farmer Benson. 'And I have a few questions for you which need answering urgently about this show.'

But then Wally raised a weary hand and cried, 'No more questions . . .' And then he roared the last words at us: 'Strictly Evacuees *is* suspended until further notice!'

CHAPTER TWENTY-EIGHT

'This is All Your Fault'

Izzy

The next few hours were the maddest of all.

After Wally's incredible announcement, Zac, Leo, Harriet and myself were told by Farmer Benson to have our tea at the farmhouse. I think Harriet was a bit annoyed at being lumped with us kids— she was seventeen, after all. But she came with us, while Miss Weed, Farmer Benson and a still very dishevelled-looking Wally went into a huddle.

In the kitchen the four of us sat eating this grey, wartime food, just as if nothing had happened and we were still on the show. But were we? Had Wally just had a hissy fit? And could he stop the whole show anyway?

Then Farmer Benson appeared. He looked grim.

'Are we still being filmed?' asked

Harriet.

'No, all filming has been suspended,' Farmer Benson said. 'But no more questions right now, please. There are meetings going on all over the place.' Then his wife bobbed in and looked as if she was about to ask him something. But he shook his head at her too. 'I can't say anything right now,' he muttered to her.

'I hope we're still in the war,' said Zac anxiously.

'I think we're all about to be chucked out and sent home,' said Leo.

'Oh no, I really don't want to do that,' said Zac.

Finally Wally appeared. He wasn't wearing his gown any more and his face looked as rumpled as an unmade bed. But his eyes still burned furiously as he spat his words out at us: 'I have come to a decision, which Reality Plus has entirely agreed with. Your constant appalling behaviour has made it impossible for the evacuation experience to continue.'

We were all stunned at this news, never really believing the show would *just splutter to an end.*

Wally continued, 'This is entirely your fault. You refused to obey the rules of wartime Britain.'

'No, we didn't,' I replied. 'We refused to obey the rules of Strictly Evacuees, which is something quite different.'

Wally's face started to turn crimson. 'Far too many rules have been broken for this experiment to continue,' he said firmly. 'But we hope to resume the show later, with a completely new set of contestants. You will all stay here tonight and the company will arrange your travel home first thing tomorrow. Your parents have been informed and will meet you at Paddington station tomorrow.' Then he added, with a withered little smile, 'Of course none of you have won our holiday prize. And tonight's events and outbursts will not be broadcast on our Strictly Evacuees highlights show. Instead, we shall issue a statement saying you were unable to deal with life as an evacuee so we're letting you all go.'

'Which is a total lie,' I said. 'But what does one more of those matter?'

Wally was, without doubt, the angriest

person I'd ever met. He was almost permanently furious. But now a gale force of rage shot through him as he shrieked, 'I left teaching some time ago because of the decline in manners, but I had a dream of bringing young people back to basic values of politeness and good behaviour. However, you have defeated even me.'

And with that he disappeared. There was a silence for a moment. Then Leo said, 'I think what Mr Cheery Chuckles means is that we've won. And he said he'd break us.' But it didn't feel like a victory at all.

Then Zac piped up, 'The show's finishing all because of me, isn't it? I should have just gone when I was told.'

'No, you shouldn't,' said a firm voice. 'Reality Plus went too far tonight—and now they are paying the consequences.' It was Miss Weed. She went on, 'I also looked forward to reacquainting modern children with old-time manners— something I firmly believe they need— but not to playing tricks on them. I really should have spoken up before. I'm very glad you two did tonight.'

Then she left too. She was a dry old stick who could be a total pain, but I sort of respected her and was actually sorry she'd gone. And knowing that Leo and I had done the right thing didn't stop me feeling horribly flat, especially as we'd all creep back home as failures now—people who just couldn't cope with being an evacuee.

That's how we'd be branded anyway.

I think Farmer Benson knew we were all feeling a bit down as he bounced in and said he wouldn't be able to get hold of any modern technology—like a television—until tomorrow. But he was going to make our last night here a very special one.

So we put on our normal clothes again—all except Zac, who said he preferred his evacuee clothes, and Mrs Benson announced, 'The bathroom is now open to the public once more.' And the room, which had been locked all through the evacuation experience, now gleamed and shone in a wonderful 2009 way.

There was no more rationing either—we could eat what we wanted. And as we didn't do any homework that night we had a joke-telling competition instead. The prize was one big bar of glorious chocolate. You can probably guess who won too: Leo, although Harriet came a very close second.

Later Farmer Benson told us his story. His farm had been struggling to make enough money for a while now. They'd started opening up the place for school visits and even having some people stay for bed and breakfast. But money was still very tight. So when Reality Plus wanted to 'borrow' his farm, it had seemed a heaven-sent piece of luck.

'How much money do you think you'll get now?' asked Leo. 'Do you have to do this again with a new group of evacuees?'

Farmer Benson gave a small smile. 'Now there's a question or two.' Later he went off to check on the animals. Of course none of us had any chores to do now, but Zac said he'd like to help. Farmer Benson looked pleased about that. And he and Zac were gone for ages.

At one point Leo went off to offer to

help too ('keenly hoping they'll say no,' he added), but he quickly came back again. 'Farmer Benson and Zac are just sitting outside the barn talking,' he said, 'so I've left them to it.'

CHAPTER TWENTY-NINE

The New Evacuee

Zac

'I shall really miss having you to help me do the chores,' said Farmer Benson. We were sitting outside the barn when he said that. And I realized that this was my chance. I felt he might be a little bit alarmed though, if I just blurted out that I wished to stay here until I was grown up. Probably better to build up to that. So at first, I asked if Victor was still visiting the farm tomorrow.

'Oh, yes,' said Farmer Benson. 'That wasn't just a stunt for the cameras. I really want to see Victor back here in his old home.'

'So do I,' I said. 'That's why I was wondering if I could stay on and watch this moment of history too.'

'Well, I don't see why not,' said Farmer Benson, 'only you'd be here as my guest.'

I nodded eagerly.

'I'll have to check with your father first, of course.'

'Oh, he's still away in Paris and my Aunt Sara won't mind at all. In fact, she'll be delighted.'

Farmer Benson looked a bit surprised at this and said gently. 'I think you might be surprised at how much your Aunt Sara has missed you.'

'No, I won't,' I said firmly, 'because it's not at all; just as I haven't missed her at all either.'

Farmer Benson frowned, and then said, 'Well, if your family agree, you can certainly stay on tomorrow. Anyway, I know Victor would be disappointed if you weren't here.'

I went on, 'Actually, if it's all right with you, what I'd really like is to stay on here'—and I really had meant to say 'a few more days', but I got so excited I cried out—'a few more years.' Then, as Farmer Benson looked totally stunned, I added hastily, 'Of course you haven't got to adopt me or anything. No, I'll just live here as Victor did before, as an evacuee. A new evacuee is what I'll call myself. And don't worry; I'll work so hard for you . . .' Then as Farmer Benson was still gazing at me in a very shocked kind of way I got up. 'Of course you'll want to have a word with Mrs Benson about this. So I'll go and have a look at the pigs for five minutes, and will it be all right if I come into the farmhouse for your decision then?' And as even then he didn't answer, I said, 'So that's what I'll do then. See you in five minutes. Cheerio for now.'

'Now just wait a moment here,' cried Farmer Benson, finding his voice at last. 'We've suddenly started travelling along at two hundred miles an hour. One moment you're asking if you can stay on here for an extra day, and the next you're saying you want to live here for a few more years.' He stood up suddenly and I thought for one awful

212

moment he was going to walk off. But instead he rubbed his hands together. 'What a day this has been . . . what a day.' Then he turned to me. 'A horrible thing happened to you tonight. Right out of the blue you heard you were going to be evicted—for nothing. So you're feeling a bit unsettled, but in the morning after a good night's sleep you'll see things differently.'

'Excuse me contradicting you, but I've been planning to live here with you for days actually. And I was just trying to pick the right moment to inform you.'

'Well, I'm very glad you finally did,' said Farmer Benson. 'And you've paid my wife and me a huge compliment tonight. But there are a few things I need to ask you first.'

'I understand,' I said. 'You want to know if I can earn my keep.'

He laughed suddenly. 'You're a funny lad,' he said.

'Everyone says that,' I agreed.

'But you're a very good lad too and it's been a pleasure having you about the place.'

'Has it really?' I said eagerly. 'I'm so very glad about that.'

Farmer Benson laughed again, but he looked kind of sad too. And then he asked me tons of questions about me and my family. I'd told him little bits before in all the chats we'd had together, but now I could feel him really listening to me.

And at the end I said, 'Well, you know far more about me than your grandad did about Victor and Dennis when they arrived here.'

'That's true enough,' he said. 'In fact, the evacuees stood in a line and local people just picked the ones they liked the look of. That's how Victor and Dennis ended up here. Times have changed a bit since then though.' He got up. 'Now let me think about all this—but don't worry, Zac, I'll look after you.'

That made me feel so full of hope.

CHAPTER THIRTY

A Final Shock

Izzy

I must have slept for about five seconds that night as Harriet and I sat up talking for hours and hours. I'd been a little bit wary of her at first. Well, just when I thought I knew all about Harriet she'd gone and turned herself into someone quite different. But we quickly got on and she kept apologizing for the things she'd done to wind me up.

Harriet said, 'Wally kept whispering to me: "Strictly Evacuees don't think you're being annoying enough." And it was quite hard thinking up new things. That's why I pretended you snored.'

'I was really upset about that.'

'I know. Sorry.'

'I'll forgive you, if you just say it one more time; the most irritating sentence in the history of the entire world.'

Harriet laughed and then yelled, 'It's

all good, babe, all good.'

In the morning Mrs Benson prepared us a superb breakfast; she broke egg after egg into the frying pan (we all had to eat at least two each), tomatoes, and then bacon, sausages, beans . . . I'd never in my life enjoyed eating more. To have food which had some flavour again seemed like an incredible treat. But I couldn't eat as much as I wanted. I'm sure my stomach had shrunk while I was being an evacuee. Then this car pulled up to take us to the station. Only Zac wasn't coming with us. Farmer Benson said Zac was staying behind to meet Victor again.

But when we asked Zac for his address and phone number, he said, 'Just contact the farm. I'll still be here . . . but don't say anything. It's a secret for now.'

'You're really going to stay on here,' I said. And Zac nodded, grinning from ear to ear.

'What do you think?' I asked Leo a bit later.

'It's what he really wants,' said Leo. 'And as he fits in here better than at his aunt's house, why not?'

When the taxi pulled away I felt a huge lump in my throat as I said goodbye—not to just Farmer and Mrs Benson (and I'd got to really like her) and poor little Zac, but to all my dreams of fame, money and a dream holiday too. Coming here had been the biggest adventure of my life. Yet now I felt as if I'd achieved exactly nothing. Mum and I were, in fact, exactly where we were before.

And I felt a bit cheated that I hadn't seen the evacuee adventure through. I'd like to have found out what the very special group challenge Wally had mentioned was going to be. And although I'd hated being bossed about and all the endless chores, I'd really liked testing myself—and sharing it all with such great friends.

Now everything was over.

A woman from Strictly Evacuees came with us on the train. She was the one we'd seen yesterday when Harriet was supposed to leave. When I asked her about our mobiles she just gazed at us stonily and said they had been *handed over to our families. She wasn't in the least bit friendly.*

Later, Harriet, Leo and I all fell asleep. I didn't wake up until the train pulled into Paddington station. And all I could think of was my mum. I couldn't wait to see her again.

Next I remember stumbling off the train, still a bit bleary-eyed from being asleep. And then Harriet suddenly calling out, 'Look!'

And there waiting for us weren't just our families—no, the whole place was crammed and roaring with reporters and other people yelling out stuff, and flashbulbs exploding while we raced towards our families.

Mum hugged me hard, and then she showed me the front page of one of the newspapers. Plastered across was a picture of us evacuees with the headline:

CHILDREN STOP REALITY SHOW. TELEVISION HISTORY WAS MADE LAST NIGHT WHEN A GROUP OF CHILDREN DEFIED A REALITY SHOW TO STAND UP FOR THEIR FRIEND.

'But how . . . ?' I burst out excitedly. 'I mean, Strictly Evacuees *didn't* broadcast any of this on the show.'

'Ah yes, but enough people had already watched it live on their computers,' said Mum.

'Oh, I'd forgotten about that,' I cried.

'And then there have been so many discussions on the internet about it ever since,' went on Mum.

'People have been discussing us?' I whispered incredulously.

I couldn't believe it. I'd thought it was all over. But no, my mad roller coaster ride was still going on. And now I'd ended up at Paddington station, surrounded by the press and people shrieking 'Well done!' and 'Congratulations!' at me. And then Mum was telling me how someone from the BBC was here to whisk us off to the studios, as we were all going to appear on the news.

'Whoa, this can't be real,' I cried. 'This is mad, amazing. It must be another trick from Strictly Evacuees.' But then I saw the woman from Strictly Evacuees slink past us, hissing anxiously into a mobile. Leo called over to me, 'The world has gone crazy, as my mum's just said I've done something right. In fact, she says we're kind of heroes. And if that doesn't make you laugh for a week, nothing will.' He punched the air. 'Come on!' he cried. 'Come on!' I grinned at him, but I couldn't speak. It was all just overwhelming.

Then Harriet tried to introduce me to her boyfriend: a tall, blond-haired guy in a leather jacket called Jeremy. But there was only time to say 'Hi' as we were half running to the BBC cars now, with Mum's arm firmly round me. And then there was another surprise—a brilliant one. Waiting by the cars were Barney and Solly. I hugged both of them madly.

'Are you coming to the studio too?' I asked.

'We couldn't miss out on this,' said Barney. 'And trust you to have all the fun after we'd gone. Then Solly whispered in my ear, 'I was cheering you on yesterday. You're mint.' And as we dived into the cars Barney asked suddenly, 'Where's Zac?'

I explained about him staying on—and then wondered, was something incredible about to happen to him too? Was his dream of living permanently on that farm about to come true?

I so hoped it was.

CHAPTER THIRTY-ONE

Another Reunion

Zac

I was waiting so impatiently for Victor.

A huge table of food had been prepared in his honour. No wartime rationings either. I was allowed to sample the cake. And it seemed so long since I'd tasted chocolate cake, I had to try a second piece as well. Mrs Benson was sure Victor wouldn't mind.

I stared at the huge banner which said: WELCOME HOME VICTOR. How incredible to return home after more than sixty years!

The farm itself seemed very quiet. I

was surprised how much I missed the other evacuees, especially Leo. 'Whenever I want to do Number Two in the night,' he'd said to me, 'I'll think of you.' I would definitely invite him to come and visit. And he could have all his holidays here on the farm. My farm.

Then I heard a taxi draw up. 'Is that Victor?' I asked.

Farmer Benson looked out of the window. He seemed surprisingly anxious. He gave me a tense smile. 'You go and be the greeter.' I think Farmer Benson had suddenly gone rather shy. Who'd have thought it?

'Of course I will,' I said. 'And don't worry, everything will be great. Well, you know how easy Victor is to get along with.'

I tore outside. I thought Victor would be pleased I was still in my evacuee clothes. He'd say . . . Then I froze in horror. I couldn't believe it. It wasn't Victor getting out of that car—it was my dad.

And in a flash I saw all my dreams just rush away. I couldn't really escape my old life, could I? Farmer Benson had just been humouring me, no doubt saying, 'I'll tell the boy anything until his dad takes him off our hands.'

And now I was being sent back to the same miserable existence as before.

'What are you doing here? You should be in Paris?' I shouted crossly at my dad. I'm not normally so rude, but right then I felt all tight and hollow inside.

'I never went to Paris in the end,' said Dad. 'Been a bit under the weather actually.' He gave a nervous smile. 'You've got some colour in your cheeks at last.' But Dad looked terrible, even worse than before. His face was a deathly pale colour now. Even his hair had gone very wispy and thin. I didn't like seeing him so ill. It worried me. But he'd totally abandoned me, so he wasn't my responsibility any more. I was totally unconnected from him now.

But still he'd come to take me back to Aunt Sara's, like some miserable gaoler. Anger and pain were swamping me now; that's why I suddenly sped away from him and ran upstairs to what

I'd really believed would be my bedroom for years and years. Then I buried my face in the pillow. I didn't want to see him or anyone ever again. I just wanted to hide away here, totally on my own.

But, of course, that didn't happen. First the Bensons came in, very softly as if I was an invalid or something.

'Zac,' called Farmer Benson. 'How are you doing, lad?' Same warm friendly voice as before. But I pretended I couldn't hear him. He'd betrayed me—that's what it felt like.

Then I heard Dad's voice and Mrs Benson saying to him, 'I expect you'd like a cup of tea after your long journey.'

'That would be super,' replied my dad. Then he added, 'Could you leave Zac and me on our own for a moment, please?'

'Of course, of course,' said Farmer Benson. Then he added, 'Been such a hard worker on the farm—best worker I've ever had, in fact.'

'I know,' said Dad. 'I've been watching him, especially with his favourites: the pigs.'

'Oh, yes, he loves the pigs,' said Farmer Benson, 'and they've taken quite a shine to him too—well, I'll leave you now.'

I was so astonished at what I'd just heard Dad say that I sat up. 'You've been watching *Strictly Evacuees*?' I said incredulously.

'Practically the whole time, on my computer,' said Dad.

'Funny,' I said. 'I never thought of you having any time to watch me.'

I'd meant because he was supposed to be at meetings in Paris, but Dad's face twisted with pain at my last comment. Then he said, 'If you want to stay on here for a few days, well, the Bensons would love to have you. They told me that.'

'And you don't mind?'

He didn't answer at first, then said in a strange, low voice, 'Of course I mind, but if that's what you want . . .'

For days I'd been certain it was. Now I wasn't quite so sure. But I said loudly, as if to quieten my doubts, 'Yes, it is.'

He moved towards the door. I

thought he was going to leave. I wanted him to—and yet I didn't.

'Zac,' he said suddenly, almost yelling my name as if I were already a long, long way from him. Then he sat down on the edge of the bed. 'When I lost your mother . . .'

'When *we* lost her,' I shouted. 'When we lost her.' The anger in my voice tore around the room. 'I lost her too, you know.'

He looked really shocked. 'I know,' he said at last.

'Well, it's the first time you've mentioned it,' I said accusingly. 'And I miss her every hour of every day. I look for her sometimes too, you know, as I still think she's going to come back, and I want her to come home so much.' I swallowed a lump in my throat. 'I so want to tell her about Leo and Barney and Izzy and Harriet; I know she'd like them, especially Leo. And I want her to meet them too. I want that so much. But it can never, ever happen now.' Tears fell from my eyes and Dad jumped up to comfort me. But I immediately sprang away from him and curled myself into a ball. 'I want you to go away now,' I mumbled.

But he didn't leave. Instead, he just sat down again.

Half to myself I muttered, 'I've been so sad and unhappy and you didn't even notice, because you don't care. You just abandoned me.'

'That's not true,' he whispered.

'Yes, it is,' I murmured.

He paused and said quietly, 'Zac, when *we*'—he emphasized the word 'we' now—'lost your mum, I couldn't face anything. It just overwhelmed me. And when I thought about life without her . . . this dead, empty feeling just seemed to sink into me.'

I sat up. It was very hard to see Dad because my eyes were so blurred, but I choked out hoarsely, 'That's exactly what happened to me too. Exactly.'

Dad reached out and took my hand. I'd meant to pull away from him, but somehow I didn't. He went on, 'I know I threw myself back into work far too much. But it was all I could cope with somehow. I could lose myself in that.'

'I suppose,' I said, 'it's a bit like me

227

and the Second World War. I like it so much because it helps me forget about everything else.' Then I added, 'Victor said I got so interested in the past because I wanted to escape from the present. Is that what you were doing too?'

'Yes, that's exactly what I was doing, Zac. But I really had no idea you were so unhappy at your Aunt Sara's.'

'Well, you should have done,' I cried, very angry again for a moment and nearly—but not quite—pulling my hand away from him.

'I know that, and I'm very, very sorry; but for a while there, the pain just seemed to swallow me up. And I couldn't see anything else.'

There was a silence for a moment before I cried eagerly, 'You know what you need now, Dad, a holiday. So why not have one here? I know Farmer and Mrs Benson wouldn't mind and well, it could be really good.'

'That's an inspired idea, Zac.'

'And after the holiday, Dad,' I went on, 'we can go back to . . . Mum would want us to go home again, wouldn't she?'

Dad looked right at me. 'And we will, Zac. We will.' Then he pulled me into a hug which practically crushed me.

We went on holding onto each other until Mr Benson called up to us.

Dad and I went to the top of the stairs.

'Sorry to interrupt,' called up Mr Benson. 'But I just thought you'd like to know that your friends are on the television at this very moment.'

'Oh, excellent!' I cried.

Dad and I raced downstairs and into the living room. The last time I'd been in here we'd been sitting round having a Second World War family night. The room didn't look all that different, although there was now a large television in the corner. Farmer and Mrs Benson were standing and watching it with rapt attention. We stood alongside them.

All the evacuees—except me, of course—were being interviewed by News 24. Izzy was saying, 'And I know I've made friends for life.'

'If not even longer,' quipped Leo.

'And that's why,' went on Izzy, 'we couldn't let Zac be treated like that. He's our friend, and so we had to stand up for him.'

'Very well put,' said Farmer Benson. 'And look at them, all talking away without any sign of nerves at all. TV naturals, they are.'

'They're fantastic,' I said. 'And I'm so happy I met them.'

'You'll see them all again very soon,' said Dad, who had an arm lightly round my shoulder. That sounded exactly like a promise.

And then we heard another taxi roll up the drive.

I looked at Dad. 'That's Victor and he—'

'He was an evacuee here in 1939 and stayed for the whole of the Second World War,' interrupted Dad.

'You really have been watching me,' I said approvingly. 'I'd better go and greet him,' I added.

I got outside just as the taxi was pulling away, and Victor was looking around him with a mixture of sadness and wonderment.

Then he saw me. 'Oh, I'm very glad you're here,' he said. 'Even though I understand *Strictly Evacuees* is not.'

'No, they've gone,' I said. 'But I couldn't miss this moment of living history.'

'And I suppose I'm the living history.'

'Well, yes, you are really.'

'Good job I remembered my hearing aid today then—and my glasses.'

We grinned at each other. 'How exactly are you feeling?' I asked.

'Like a ghost,' said Victor firmly. 'And especially when I see you standing there, looking more than a bit like me and in identical clothes.'

'I wanted to be authentic,' I said proudly.

'You really are,' said Victor. 'And now time is twisting and shrinking away so much . . . well, I half expect the people who lived here all those years ago, and who were so very kind to me, to come rushing out to greet me again.'

'Wonderful if they could,' I said.

'And poor old Dennis; I'd give anything to see him tearing towards me with that big grin on his face. And I'd be thinking, what bit of mischief have you been up to now?' Victor smiled and shook his head and seemed totally lost in memories for a moment.

Then I gently took his hand. 'And now,' I said, 'I'd really like you to meet my dad.'